Unelmoija: The Dreamshifter

Elle Boca

Poyeen Publishing

Published by Poyeen Publishing
2901 Clint Moore Road #265
Boca Raton, FL 33496

ISBN: 978-1-932534-17-7

Sign up to receive news and updates about Elle Boca titles and special offers at

http://elleboca.poyeen.com/the-dreamshifter/

Other titles by Elle Boca:

Unelmoija: The Mindshifter
Unelmoija: The Spiritshifter
Unelmoija: The Timeshifter
Unelmoija: Paradox
In the Garden of Weeia
Gypsies, Tramps and Weeia
Weeia on My Mind
Smells Like Weeia Spirit

Author's Note

This is an original work of fiction. Any relationship to real people is unintentional and a coincidence. The setting is Earth and the places are for the most part real although at times I took literary liberties, modifying locations, addresses, etc. as necessary to adapt to the story.

Acknowledgements

I am deeply I'm thankful to Lourdes L. Garrido for her feedback on the early draft. The insights shared by beta readers Jennifer Martinez and Susanne Rieth were most helpful. Any mistakes are mine.

Table of Contents

To Gary

Chapter 1

A light dinner followed by a swim and a good night's rest was what I needed. I woke up full of energy, remembering no dreams. Pulling on my jogging clothes I looked in the full-length mirror. Sleepy blue eyes set in an oval face with prominent cheekbones and slightly exotic features blinked back at me. The Florida sun was starting to color my pale complexion. At five foot seven inches and one hundred and fifteen pounds, I still felt gawky and self-conscious about my slight build. At least I'd fit in with the many people I'd seen exercising around the Brickell area the day before. I filed one of my unpolished nails that had gotten snagged while bringing my stuff over the previous day. Tying my medium length dark brown hair into a ponytail I tiptoed out of the apartment to keep from waking Rosario, my new landlady. Lost in deep slumber, I hadn't heard her come in, but assumed if it had been late she was catching up on her beauty sleep. I didn't know if she was an early riser or a night owl. She had said the first thing she did when she woke up was make a pot of coffee. The kitchen was dark and there was no coffee smell. Better to leave without entering the kitchen to avoid waking her.

I headed north on the street in front of Rosario's building along the bay facing side, seeing other joggers along the way. I felt safe. This part of the city was reserved for condominiums on the south side and commercial buildings close to the Miami Downtown District. Thirty minutes into my jog, as I was getting my bearings of the area and thinking of buying bottled water at a small mart, I noticed a well-dressed man get out of a car and look in my direction.

He didn't stand out and at first I thought he might be headed to a meeting at one of the nearby bank or office buildings. I hesitated thinking he was going to ask for directions. I didn't know the area well and would be of little help. He seemed to be looking at me. He parked across the street instead of in front of the store, which made no sense. Maybe he was stopping on his way to work to pick up a cup of coffee, a muffin or something to eat, I thought. "You're being paranoid," I told myself.

Something about his face seemed familiar. He was older, about Mom's age, attractive, tall and distinguished looking. When he noticed me looking at him he smiled and I turned away. I didn't want to give this strange man the wrong impression. It was clear he was looking at me so I entered the mart, seeking the safety of the store, and bought a bottle of water. When I left the shop he was waiting for me.

"Amy, do not be frightened. It is you I came to see. If you give me a moment I will explain." His words, the unexpected familiarity and friendliness shot me with adrenaline. This man had found me, after I'd only just moved the night before, during my morning jog. I kept my distance and remained silent while I considered the situation.

Until that moment, I hadn't realized how the recent kidnapping attempt had shaken my trust in strangers. We escaped our captors under the cover of a storm, but our comfortable lives hadn't returned to normal. I didn't think he was one of the men who had taken us to the Caribbean. They acted like military men; they used physical force and veiled threats. This man looked more like an executive.

He appeared to be alone, but he might have me under discrete surveillance. If he'd been keeping tabs on me, it was better to discover his identity and agenda; but I needed a safer place than standing on the street alone before dawn.

"Who are you?" I couldn't help blurting. It would be useful to make mental note of as much as I could to describe him to Mom. I noticed he had straight brown hair that was graying in parts. He spoke without contractions, like someone who preferred formal English or spoke English as a second language. There was something deeply powerful about him. It was more than that. He looked like a man accustomed to being in charge and giving orders.

"My name is Thomas McKnight," he said.

"What do you want with me? Why are you here?" I kept my voice down, looked at his eyes.

"Please give me a few moments and I will explain. If you do not like what I say, I will leave you alone." He looked at the store and back at me. "How about if we sit inside? Would you like a cup of coffee?" It occurred to me that it had been a long time since anyone had refused his commands. He probably gave orders and people obeyed. He was going out of his way to be friendly, but I wondered for how long he'd hold back and what he wanted with me.

I entered the twenty-four hour mart and chose a table in the small coffee shop. In this ritzy neighborhood, the mart was stocked with exclusive brands and expensive merchandise. It appeared that most of the patrons lived in one of the nearby residential towers. At that hour, they were grabbing a light breakfast, out for a morning jog or walking their dogs. The occasional office worker or executive on the way to the office a few blocks north filled foam cups with coffee, and bought lottery tickets and newspapers. Although our corner of the store was deserted, there were cameras and a couple of employees who would notice if he got physical or blocked me from leaving.

He followed at a measured pace, stood in line to buy an espresso and sat down across from me at the table. I sat in silence, except for the pounding of my heart which sounded loud in my ears, while I waited for him to speak. He was the one who wanted to talk to me. Let him say what he had to say. He had a radiant smile like he'd just won the Lotto or found the fountain of youth. A dark suntan made the blue of his eyes seem intense.

Manicured hands held the cup of espresso which he drank in a long swallow without sugar or milk, just like my sister Kat. I missed her more at moments like this; she always knew what we should do in any crisis. I hoped Mom had found her and would return soon.

His well-tailored suit was expensive. Custom-made, I speculated, and the way it hung on his trim frame and his graceful movements told me he was in excellent physical condition. If I ran, he could chase me. And, he was dangerous. I could tell by looking at him he was strong and lethal. This man had killed. I didn't know how I knew but I knew it was true. There was a darkness to him that had nothing to do with the tan.

"Your mother has done a phenomenal job, better than I imagined. You are smart, cautious and have excellent self-control. And your special abilities are starting to develop," I must have reacted to the last words because he smiled at me. "Yes, I know about your abilities Amy. It is a gift you must learn to use with care but a gift to be used nonetheless," I lowered my eyes to keep him from seeing the burning curiosity and temptation they held.

"I ask you again, who are you Mr. McKnight and what do you want with me?" I figured he was going to give me some lame answer and was unprepared for his next words.

"I am your father."

As soon as the words left his mouth I knew they were true. I didn't know how I knew. I just knew. The powerful man before me was my father. Before I'd accept that statement I wanted answers. My mouth became dry, my heart raced, I felt overcome with conflicting emotions. All my life, I waited to be reunited with my father, an idealized figure perfected over the years in my mind. Here he was before me and I didn't know what to say or how to feel. I should be happy, but I wasn't. I was afraid of this man.

"You can't be my father," I said. His puzzled look made

me continue. "My father was captured years ago by our enemies. The same men who took him kidnapped my mother and me a few weeks ago."

"I was captured, but it happened before you were born," he said. I knew again he spoke the truth. "Your mother told you the truth, but not the whole story." He had ignored the revelation that we had been kidnapped; I wasn't sure what that meant. Did he know about it? Had he been involved? More than anything, I wanted to talk to my mother at that moment.

"The real question is what you want with me. Why are you here? How did you know where to find me?" I worried that I didn't dislike him and I didn't like that he knew far more about me than I knew about him. He was no less dangerous even if he was my father. The thought came unbidden.

"I wanted to meet you Amy. You are my daughter." What he said was true yet there was more he wasn't telling me. "As to how I found you … it is easy. Anytime you use your ability I feel it. You and I are linked." He sounded smug like any two-year-old would know what he was saying. I didn't know anything about my abilities or this link he was talking about. And, the father Mom had described had little to do with the man at the table with me.

"I haven't felt any link with you."

"Nonetheless, it is true. I felt you draw on your ability just two nights ago."

I thought back at my attempt to force Sarah to return the money she had stolen from us and my anger that she'd killed her own mother out of greed. It was one of my first real dreams and didn't turn out as I'd hoped. I'd been lucky afterwards to meet Officer Alicia Gomez, a policewoman willing to help rather than toss me in jail. Now it turned out that my father could trace me when I used my dream ability, better and better.

He was watching me closely and the smug expression on his face showed he knew he was right. "It seems you have no training and little knowledge about your ability and how to use it." It was my turn to look puzzled. "You are a powerful young woman Amy. It is no surprise. Your mother is powerful in her own right and so am I. I trust you know we are all Weeia, a superhuman race." A what? Come again? He kept talking while I was stuck on the part about being members of a superhuman race. Once again something told me he had spoken the truth. "You need to learn about your abilities so you can use them to your advantage. Knowledge will help you protect yourself." I didn't want to give away how little I knew. I let him continue without interrupting. I noticed he hadn't asked about Mom. It gave me a knot in my stomach. Had he done something to her?

"You experienced dreamshifting. While you are in a directed dream, focus concentration on your wish for something to change and it becomes reality if you have enough power available. All you have to do is wish it. That is rare even among Weeia." I missed some of what he was saying, letting my thoughts wonder for a moment. He could teach me about my ability. He could answer so many questions. Unfortunately, I didn't think I could trust him.

"Before that you used your abilities on a few other occasions. I noticed because you inherited this ability from me and as I said, we are linked. I am interested in what you do and in what other gifts you may have inherited." He looked at me, waiting for a response.

"Mom said using my ability was dangerous to others and to me. She said I have to be careful. I believe Mom. She wants what's best for me. You're telling me to use my ability."

"And, you do not believe or trust me." He finished the sentence with ease and his now familiar smile. "Trust your feelings Amy. How do you feel when you dreamshift? Does it feel like it is bad? Does it feel like something you want to do again?"

I couldn't deny the euphoria I felt whenever I had a real dream. The few times I'd dreamed before had been when I was afraid, powerless and threatened. My ability had made the difference between a frightened girl and a powerful young woman. The dreams had allowed me to push back at bad people who hurt me like the kidnappers and Sara, the mother killer, in an amazing, empowering way. Yes, it was true. I liked my ability. It felt good to use it. I felt drawn to use it again. Each time I dreamshifted, I wanted to do it again and try bigger things. Just because I wanted to do it again didn't mean it was good. Still, I wanted to know more about this ability and about him.

"Tell me about your abilities," I pressed him. I looked at his eyes. They were strong and full of raw energy. They drew me in. It was like I wanted to want what he wanted. I wanted to please him. Was it because he was my father? Was he using his abilities on me? I shook my head to clear it, waiting for his response.

He watched me without replying for a long time. So long I thought he wasn't going to answer my question.

"You said you wanted to meet me. It's done. You met me. If you don't want to tell me about yourself we have nothing left to talk about." I got up to leave.

"I can extend my abilities to the day, beyond dreams. With just a thought I can make people do things even if they do not want to obey me." I didn't say anything, waiting for him to continue. I knew there was more. "If I set my mind to it I know what they feel, think, want, and when something is true. As you may have noticed by now, every time you use your ability you feel tired. That is normal like being tired after jogging for an hour or swimming ten laps in the pool. With time and practice you will be better at it and feel less tired." He looked at me for confirmation. I said nothing.

"You've given me a lot to think about Mr. McKnight. I'm going to need some time to absorb all of this. Meeting you is a shock and I'm not sure I believe it," I said.

"I understand dad won't work for now. Please call me Tom." For now? Did he think he was entitled to be called "dad"?

"For now I'm fine with Mr. McKnight." He wasn't my friend. I wasn't going to fall for that false sense of closeness. Where had he been all my life? I didn't believe he cared. He wanted something from me. That was why he'd come to see me and was being all Mr. Nice. He might have his own abilities, even stronger than mine but there was a catch he wasn't sharing and there was something he wanted from me, but what was it?

"All these years while I was growing up where were you? Where was this magic link between us?" My voice was breaking with emotion. I might not trust him but I was desperate for a loving father. I'd worshiped my missing father since I was a little girl, believing he was a good man who had been wronged by bad men who held him prisoner to make him do terrible things. The truth was more complex than I'd imagined. Still, I yearned to find a kernel of truth to the idea that I had a father who loved me. What little girl didn't?

He reached for my hand. I jerked it away while wiping uncontrollable tears flowing down my cheeks. The employee of the shop turned to look at me when he saw me crying. I returned his look to let him know I was all right. It wasn't true. I was far from all right, and I was mad at myself for crying. It was a sign of weakness. At that moment, I couldn't help crying any more than I could help breathing. Sadness was expelled through every pore of my body and I shook with emotion.

With a slow deliberate movement, perhaps to keep from frightening me, he showed me his hand reaching into his jacket pocket where he withdrew a linen handkerchief he handed me. I accepted, taking a moment to compose my thoughts and calm down. I had to set my emotions aside. This man was not to be trifled with or trusted regardless of how much I wanted him to be the daddy I'd missed all those long years of hiding while I was growing up.

To his credit, he waited until I signaled numbly that he could continue saying "I am sorry I was not there. I wanted to be. Maybe we should talk about that the next time we see each other. Will you allow me to see you again?"

I ignored his question. There was something he was hiding about his abilities and I wanted to know what it was. I was curious about him and his abilities because, if what he said was true, we shared common abilities. I wanted to know what they meant and how to manage them. I didn't want him to know how little I knew. The best way to learn about my own abilities was to learn about his, I hoped.

"What aren't you telling me about your abilities?"

He looked at me intently before speaking. "You are intuitive too." A moment passed in which he seemed to lose himself somewhere else. As I thought he was going to dismiss my question he went on. "There are indeed other issues involved in using my abilities, yours too as you know. This is not the place or time to discuss such a sensitive topic. There are others like us who would use our abilities for their own purposes. We must be careful."

I felt cold. I looked down at my arm to find goose bumps. He followed my look and sprang up in front of me, startling me. "What—" I didn't have a chance to finish my question. A young man entered the shop and stood in front of us in no time. One minute we were alone and the next minute he was there.

"This is a bad idea Mr. Bittersdorp," my father said to the man, shielding me with his own body so I could almost not see the new arrival. "You have not been invited. You are bringing undesirable attention making an appearance so abruptly."

"Ask me if I care. Nobody saw me, so I didn't break the rules you stodgy old farts drew up to keep yourselves hidden. I'll do as I please and see whom I please. It's none of your concern."

While he spoke I had a chance to look at him. He was tall, thin like a runner, with curly hair, dark brown with lighter highlights, and had brown eyes with long lashes.

"Besides, I didn't come to talk to you, McKnight. She's the reason I found my way to this hell hole they call a city, hot, humid and full of impolite peons with delusions of grandeur that pass for human. What's your name little girl?" I couldn't see my father's face but his body was tense, in a fighting stance.

"Little girl? Go away; you're interrupting a private conversation." The words just flew out of me almost of their own volition. I didn't like this guy. My father didn't like this guy. Was that influencing my feelings? Maybe but I was pretty sure the dislike was mine as well. Something about him rubbed me the wrong way. It wasn't so much that I was afraid; I could tell he was dangerous, but that wasn't it, as that his presence bothered me. Something about him repelled me the way a bad smell made me want to walk away. I didn't want anything to do with him. His being there was uncomfortable. I wanted him to leave.

I turned away from him and after a while he got the message. Without a word he disappeared just as he first appeared. In the same way I had known he was nearby before I saw him I knew he was gone.

I let my curiosity loose. "Who was that man?"

"Duncan Bittersdorp is his name. He has little respect for the rules and his betters. Be careful if you see him again. I do not like that he has taken an interest in you. Has he approached you before?"

I nodded my head from side to side while I thought. "No, I'd remember that unpleasant feeling. Is that normal?"

"Your mom did not explain the batjar to you?" It was more a statement than a question. I said nothing. There were so many things I wanted Mom to explain. Why had she kept this from me?

"When polar opposites are near, they repel each other. He is your polar opposite which is why you could feel him before you saw him. He has the same reaction to you that you have to him. It is also the reason I was surprised to see him seek you out."

"You're not as powerful and all mighty as you want me to think. This younger guy snuck up on us and you didn't notice until I did." Somehow knocking him down a peg made me feel better, less afraid of him.

"You are right. I should have been aware. I should have noticed his presence before you did. Having a security detail has made me soft." Was that a touch of shame in his voice? "I was distracted answering your questions and did not—well it does not matter. He is of no consequence."

In one morning, I learned more about my father than in most of my life. I needed time to digest everything he said, that I belonged to another race of people who had special abilities and the knowledge about an ability I shared with my long lost father. I also had to figure out why my mother had lied to me most of my life. I should be angry with her. I wasn't. I knew that whatever Mom had done was to protect Kat and me. If she'd kept things from us about our father she had her reasons, I was sure of it. I couldn't wait for her to return.

"He must have followed you. I just moved. No one knows about me or where I am. You found me with that special power link but how would he have known about me or where to find me? What does he want with you?"

"Like I said before, you are not just a pretty face. There is a disagreement between The Elders and many of the younger generations." The Elders? That seemed so archaic. I had other fish to fry so I better pay attention, I told myself.

"He seemed eager to talk to me. What do you think he wants?" I said.

"I do not know." I got the feeling those words didn't pass his lips often. Duncan Bittersdorp had caught him by surprise and that was making my father uncomfortable. "There are rumors of a revolution among the youth. For years their leaders have been lobbying The Elders for changes in our laws."

"You want something from me. I can sense that. That's why you're here today. What is it?" I could almost see the thoughts crossing his mind. He thought of denying it, playing the lost father card. Then he thought being honest would win my approval. He went with that.

"Amy, I am your father. Even though we do not know each other the way I would like I care about you. I regret not finding you before." That rang true but incomplete.

"Let us spend some time together another day this week. We can go to the park or have lunch. Whatever you want." He sounded tentative. Maybe he'd never spoken to a teenage daughter before. "It will give us a chance to get to know each other and I can answer your questions." I appreciated his willingness to give me time although I didn't trust him much. The part about being my father was true. At the same time, he didn't have my best interests at heart.

"All I am asking you to do for now is to see me and get to know me. You can decide the rest later. How does that sound?" I needed time to think, process what he said, find out more about him, talk to Mom, find out about this Weeia race he said we belonged to, and ask my mother why she kept him and my abilities hidden from me.

"Okay. How do I reach you?"

"You can think about me and our link or use your

dreamshifting ability and you can find me any time." I noticed he didn't offer to help if Duncan Bittersdorp accosted me. "I understand that may not feel comfortable now so we can use a more conventional means of communication." He handed me a prepaid cell phone with his phone number in it. "Call me tomorrow and let me know where you want to go. Anytime, anyplace." He must be a busy guy and he was letting me pick the time and place.

"This is a lot to absorb. I need more time to think. How about I call you the day after tomorrow?"

"Deal." He wasn't happy but he didn't push. Good for him or maybe it was good for me.

I watched him walk to his car and drive away, waiting another thirty minutes, like Mom had taught me to do to avoid being followed. I left the mart heading in the opposite direction to make sure I didn't lead him back to Rosario's building. Maybe his link was approximate and not exact. I didn't know if he could tell exactly where to find me or the general area where I was. In case it was approximate I preferred to keep my new address to myself since he had led the other guy straight to me. Mom wouldn't be happy. Then again, Mom had a lot of explaining to do. I'd call her as soon as I had a private moment. She'd be distressed by the news. Besides, what I'd told my father was true. I needed time to process the new information.

Chapter 2

As I turned the corner, walking away from the mart and about to continue my interrupted morning jog, I felt the strange sensation I'd felt earlier and goose bumps appeared all over my body. I braced myself for an attack that didn't come.

"You must be important." It was half question and half statement.

"Why do you say that?"

"He protected you when I arrived. The dodgy old fart doesn't protect anyone unless there's something in it for him too. He has no time to spare and yet he's here, meeting with you, little girl, in the butt of the country where there are no satellites. Why is that? Who are you?" He approached me as if that would make me answer him.

My skin still crawled from his nearness but I stood my ground. It bothered me but I knew it bothered him too. "You're rather rude. You interrupted our conversation without as much as a 'good morning' or 'hi, my name is Duncan.' Why should I tell you anything?"

That seemed to take him back. He studied me before saying "Hi, my name is Duncan. It's a pleasure, well not entirely a pleasure because of the batjar, to meet you. And you are? If you don't tell me your name I'll just call you little girl." For some reason little girl bothered me. I opted for the lesser evil.

"Amy."

"Amy what?"

"Just Amy."

"Okay Just Amy. It's a not-pleasure to meet you. What did that old fart McKnight want?"

"I don't know. He wouldn't say. He did say to stay away

from you because you wanted something. Why were you looking for me? Do you want something?"

"Everybody wants something Just Amy. I wanted to talk to him and ran into you by accident. Now I just want to know why you're important to McKnight and The Elders. Once I know what makes you important to them I may want something. Now, I don't want anything." While he spoke I made a point of looking closely at him. "The more you know the better you can protect yourself," Mom's words popped up in my head. He had an intense look. A thin long scar crossed his face. Maybe I'd mistaken it for cruelty. He was older than I thought at first glance; in his late twenties or early thirties even.

"You told him you were looking for me."

"I lied. It's always good to keep the old goat guessing. Besides, why should I tell him anything?"

"I see." I stalled while I thought of a question. I might not have another opportunity to speak with this man.

"No you don't see." His tone turned serious. "McKnight is trouble. You shouldn't have met with him. Whatever he wants won't be good for you or for anyone. Besides, a young girl like you shouldn't meet with a dangerous Elder like him outside the presence of her parents."

This age thing was starting to bother me; I'm young looking for my age, but seriously. "For your information, I'm eighteen years old and can talk to anyone I like. And what do you know about McKnight?"

"I know he's a senior Elder. I know he's selfish and dangerous and capable of manipulating reality and people. He's powerful and one of the leaders who has squashed our movement. He's said to be responsible for the deaths of dozens, including a few who were just old enough to be coming into their abilities. Stay away from him for your own good." I didn't like strangers telling me what to do. Who did he think he was?

"Not that it's your concern, I didn't ask to meet him. He found me. And, who I meet with is none of your bees wax. You don't know me. You don't know anything about me. If I live or die, see him or not what do you care anyway?" I said feeling smug.

"I may not know you but I know some things about you. You're more like me than you are like him. You don't like him either. If you did you would have defended him and you haven't. It's not that you want to see him. It's that just on principle you don't like me telling you not to see him. If I use reverse psychology and tell you to see him maybe it'll work better." There was an irritating smile on his face when he stopped talking. He was cute, handsome even, when he wasn't annoying me with advice.

"Well..."

"So, Just Amy, where are you headed?" Before I could deny he was right his lighthearted tone returned.

"I'd like to finish my jog if it's okay with you." I tried sounding annoyed but I couldn't muster up the energy. He didn't seem that bad now that I'd spoken with him a couple of minutes. I was getting used to the batjar. "What's your ability anyway?" I said to make conversation more than anything.

"I can move fast, real fast. So fast, most people, even The Elders, can't see me."

"Sounds like fun."

"It can be. Wanna try?"

I shrugged, unsure. Next thing I knew he stood behind me and hugged me. He was taller than I was; his touch was unexpected, gentle. The not-pleasant feeling was still there though now it felt like a buzzing in the background. I turned my head to the right but I couldn't see his face from so close. "Don't be afraid. It doesn't hurt. Ready?" I started nodding before I realized we were moving, people, cars, buildings, plants, everything was a blur. When we stopped I looked around. We were two blocks away from where we had been standing. I only knew because I'd noticed the bright green restaurant awning at one of the buildings earlier and it stood just two feet away from where we were at that moment.

"What do you think? You dizzy, lightheaded, nauseous, tired, have a headache, trouble breathing?" Duncan stood in front of me, looking at me with concern.

"Nope. No to all of that. I feel fine. I feel better than fine. It was awesome." I was smiling. It had been great. What a fun power to have. "Do it again?"

"Only if you have breakfast with me. There's a place in Little Havana that makes delicious Cuban sandwiches and fab fruit shakes. That's my price." The serious guy was gone and in his place was a younger, more playful person, almost carefree. Maybe I should opt out, be safe. "I don't have enough money for breakfast. I only brought enough cash for a bottle of water and a muffin and I spent it already." I hadn't bought the muffin but the excuse was valid if I wanted one.

"Healthy I see." There was the smile from before. It changed his face, making him look younger and more likable. "That won't get you off the hook Just Amy. I'm treating. Anyway, this place isn't expensive. And who knows you might not like it. Naw, that's not possible. Their food is so good even a spoiled teenager like you will like it. What do you say?"

Before I said much of anything he'd resumed his place behind me, placing strong muscular arms around my waist and whispering in my ear "Don't worry. We're just going for breakfast. I'll bring you back anytime you want me to." I couldn't say no. It had been so much fun and I was curious. Besides, he seemed nice enough in spite of the not-pleasant batjar feeling. I nodded yes and we were off. This time our walk was longer than the first two blocks had been. I couldn't be sure but it seemed to me Duncan was moving with extra care. I never felt jostled or uncomfortable. I didn't know exactly where in Little Havana we were going but I knew Little Havana was near, in relative terms, to Brickell, the upscale neighborhood where Rosario's apartment and my new temporary home were located. I had read about Little Havana in the tourist guides. Once, many Cuban exiles had called the area home. These days residents tended to be from Central America. It retained, according to the guidebooks, much of the character and charm of its early days and was worth a visit.

When we stopped the neighborhood looked different from Brickell. Where that area was full of tall towers, a mix of offices and condominiums, this area had few tall structures of any kind. It looked more modest, even run down.

Again Duncan stood in front of me, looking at me with concern. "You dizzy, lightheaded, nauseous, tired, have a headache, trouble breathing?"

"None of the above. I'm hungry. Where's that delicious breakfast you promised?" Duncan looked puzzled. "You sure? Do you feel any discomfort of any kind?"

"I like your fast fabulous strolling. No discomfort except for that opposites buzz I feel when you're near me. Are you trying to chicken out of your promise?"

"It was my price for another faster than fast fabulous stroll with me. Since you're feeling well and prepared to pay the price, so shall we go to breakfast. Follow me."

"What, walk like a regular person?" I laughed. "No speedy walk?"

"It's around the corner Just Amy. It won't take but a moment to get there. You're not getting lazy after only two short fast fabulous strolls, as you call them, are you?"

"Not a chance. Are you getting worn out?"

"I'm ready to eat, salivating at the thought of a good breakfast. I should warn you this place isn't fancy and it can get loud, real loud though at this hour it shouldn't be too bad. How's your Spanish? *Habla español*?"

"Muy poquito, siñor. You?"

"I can order." By then we had arrived. He opened the door and waved me through. It was full; making me think breakfast would have to wait until someone left. A plump dark haired woman wearing a tight fitting uniform and lots of makeup greeted us in Spanish. Duncan answered in accented Spanish and she led us to a table in the back. Before she left he spoke to her and she answered yes in Spanish.

"What did you say?" It was necessary to yell it was so loud. It was not a good place for conversation. I wouldn't be able to ask him any questions but then again he wouldn't be able to ask me any either. Maybe that was why he picked that place. It would keep the awkwardness down.

"If we wait for her to bring us menus to order it will be another twenty minutes and someone said she was hungry. I took the liberty of ordering a little food and two fruit shakes; they make them with milk here, extra thick. When the menus arrive you can order more."

I looked around, curious to see the people and the restaurant. The décor was simple although clean, and judging by the many empty plates, patrons were hungry or enthusiastic about the food. Our table had paper place mats, inexpensive cutlery, empty glasses and cups and bread plates. Before long a man brought us menus as well as two glasses of iced water, a basket of warm bread and a bowl with individually wrapped butter containers. We fell on the bread like locusts. I've never seen locust in person, only in videos online, and they eat with similar speed and less frenzy.

Thinking Duncan had ordered just bread, butter and a snack, I opened a menu. It was in Spanish with imperfect English language translations underneath each item in small type. There were the usual breakfast items I was familiar with and several exotic versions like one dish, *Bistec a Caballo* described as an egg atop a steak or egg on horseback. There were soups, sandwiches, appetizers, and mains. Duncan explained the mains were only available after 11 a.m. There were also desserts, fresh juices, fruit and regular shakes and several kinds of coffee like *Cortadido* and *Cubano*. Not being a coffee drinker I skipped back to the sandwiches. I was getting ready to pick one when the waitress arrived with two large thick sandwiches, hot off the grill, and a plate each of fried plantains and fried something else I didn't recognize.

She asked if we needed anything else, Duncan explained. I decided that was enough food for the moment and asked Duncan which sandwich was for me. He said I could try both and choose a favorite. I bit into one hot half sandwich and fell in love. It was the kind of flavorful, satisfying comfort food I liked on special occasions. It had generous quantities of ham, pork, Swiss cheese, butter, mayo and pickles stuffed between two slices of crunchy Cuban bread. Diet food it was not but it was delicious with capital letters. The other sandwich had a similar filling within somewhat sweet less crunchy bread. I liked both. If I had to choose one the first one won the contest. The fried crunchy plantains and fried cassava, Duncan had explained in between bites that the second plate of fried food was cassava, a pale root vegetable similar to potatoes, were divine. The only problem was I had no room left for dessert. Duncan suffered no such problem. He ordered another sandwich, plantains and French fries and a second shake, then had two desserts followed by a strong and sweet Cuban coffee chaser.

By the time he was on the second half of his second sandwich it was less noisy and I could hear him when he spoke inches from my ear. "One of the benefits of using my ability is that I can eat as much as I want and never gain weight." It was obvious watching him that he enjoyed this eating benefit to the max. I smiled.

I could understand the initial attraction of unlimited eating.

A Hollywood star would kill for it. I guessed Duncan had to eat often and a lot to support his fast fabulous strolling abilities. I was learning that the advantage of our abilities brought with it a down side. Maybe in his case, eating a lot was the only disadvantage. It didn't seem to bother him.

By the time we left the restaurant I was wishing I'd finished my jogging circuit that morning. Turning to Duncan as we stood on the side street I said, "Thanks for breakfast and bringing me here. That was yummalicious."

"It was a pleasure for me Just Amy. You're nice to be with. Where would m'lady like to go now?" he bowed low. When he rose there was an impish look on his face.

"Well, it's my first time in Little Havana. I've read about it and would love seeing a little of it. Can we walk for a while?"

"Sure Just Amy. I have time if you have time. *Mi Little Havana es su Little Havana.*"

It was the first time in days that I was just having fun, walking and sightseeing for no reason without worrying, too much, that a potential kidnapper was around the corner. I hadn't realized until she went out of town how much I relied on Mom for support, guidance, company and feeling safe. Without Mom to watch my back I had been tense, anxious and grumpy all the time, and lonely. Now, I felt relief almost as a tangible thing. Duncan was good company and I felt safe with him. I had a feeling no one would bother me while we were together.

I'd seen his serious, dangerous side first. Although I liked this fun side better the dangerous side made me feel protected. My day was brighter for the short while we had been together. He might want something from me like my father had said but if he did he was in no hurry to get it. Duncan hadn't even asked what my abilities were even after I asked about his.

We walked around, entering exotic *botanicas* that sold

potions, statues of saints and magical ingredients, Spanish language only bookstores and anything that looked interesting or different. We stopped to watch elderly men playing at Domino Park, bought *mamey* (a tropical sweet fruit) shakes for Duncan and joked around. Our time together was ending and I was dreading saying good bye. I figured Duncan had to go to work or deal with something related to the voting meeting my father had mentioned was so important. It must have shown on my face because he began to tease me. I said everything was fine. He said even after knowing me only for a few hours he could tell something was on my mind. I couldn't quite tell him everything Mom and I had gone through. I didn't know what he knew or if he knew about Mom. I wasn't sure what was okay for us to talk about but I didn't want to lie to him. He started clowning around to "rescue my smile" and soon I was laughing up a storm.

"Hey, Just Amy. Have you been to South Beach? If you think I was a good Little Havana guide I'm a killa South Beach guide. What do you say to lunch in South Beach? Oh, I can see a bright light in your eyes. Is that a smile peeking out at me?"

The next thing I knew he was wrapping his arms around me and we were heading toward South Beach. On the way we stopped at the Causeway, the bridge that connects the mainland to Miami Beach, Duncan explained, to watch the cruise ships at the Port of Miami. Of course, Duncan had a favorite restaurant there too. We didn't have reservations and even at lunch the restaurant was crowded. We waited a few minutes and were rewarded with a table with a view of the water. The thing to order there, he offered, was stone crabs. Available only part of the year they drew fans from all corners of the globe, he told me after the waiter took our order. It was best to get them in a middle size, not too small and not jumbo either.

Lunch was as satisfying as breakfast although that restaurant was much pricier than the modest place in Little Havana. "Don't worry about the price, Just Amy. It's my treat. I work hard and make good money but I don't make time to go for a meal for pleasure often. This is a special treat for me."

Duncan ordered copious quantities of the crabs, sold by the pound at varying prices depending on the size. It sounded like so much I was afraid we wouldn't be able to finish them. The piles of crab claws looked like a lot of food when the server brought them. Soon I discovered they looked big because they came in the shell and we had to work to get the meat out. The kitchen cooked and cracked the claws just enough for us to do the rest. We could eat them as they were served or dip them in drawn butter or mustard sauce. I tasted all three and decided I liked the natural flavor of the claws best. As I looked up from my crab tasting experiment I saw Duncan look at me, an amused expression on his face.

"What's so funny Fastman?" Fastman had become my official nickname for Duncan and he seemed to like it. At first he fought it but the last few times he hadn't said anything.

"You. . . you take your food so seriously. We're turning the whole opposites concept on its ear you and I. Despite the not pleasant buzzing in the background we have a lot of things in common."

I didn't know anything other than what my father had said about opposites. I wasn't sure what Duncan meant. "I know what you mean. In spite of your cheeky attitude we do seem to get along." He laughed, reaching for another crab. "There's more. I can't describe it exactly. I feel connected to you in an odd way. It's like we repel and attract each other at the same time. I thought opposites didn't get along. Do you know any opposites who spend time together?"

"No, I haven't heard of any. Just the opposite, no pun intended, I thought there were few and they didn't get along. You're the first time I meet an opposite of mine." His face turned serious. "Can I tell you a secret?" He waited to see if I objected to the secret before going on. "It's more than getting along. You're one of the few people I've ever been able to take on long speed strolls. After a couple of blocks they usually get sick. The symptoms are different. Some get bad headaches, others have trouble breathing or get nauseous or dizzy. The thing is they don't do well. You don't seem to have a bad reaction at all. Do you?"

"Naw, you're just trying to wiggle out of showing me South Beach, trying to scare me into going home because you aint the killa tour guide you said you were. And, you're afraid I'll figure it out and the game will be up."

"I'm serious Amy. Does strolling with me give you any symptoms? Have you felt nauseous, dizzy, a headache, anything?"

"Does overfull count?" He laughed and threw his crab stained wet napkin at me.

"Ew. Keep your napkin to yourself Speedy." I also called him Speedy and he hadn't objected to that at all. "And stay away from my crab claws. I'm still eating." Not for long I knew but it was fun to tease him.

"Well?" he wasn't going to let up until I answered his question.

"No, Duncan, fast walking with you today has been wonderful. Except for the buzzing you know about I feel great. I love the strolling and I enjoy your company lots. This has been the most fun I've had in several weeks. Now enough of that before your ego gets bigger than it already is."

Later, when we were walking around Lincoln Road, a popular pedestrian street, Duncan told me how different I was from other Weeia he knew. "You were willing to visit a new place, try new food, and stroll with me after meeting me for the first time, not because you wanted anything. You weren't after my abilities or asking me for anything. Others with abilities are looking for an advantage, money, position or want to show off that their ability is better than yours. Do you know how refreshing it is to be with you?"

"I was a bit afraid. You were confrontational and seemed dangerous when you showed up at the mart this morning. I wasn't sure what to expect. I had a feeling it would be safe and took a chance. I haven't met many people with abilities Duncan."

At a small shop with things crammed in every corner, even dangling from the ceiling we met the eccentric owner when I kept her from falling after an angry customer brushed by her without paying attention to her frail frame. She was a psychic, she said, and wanted to repay my kindness. I replied no payment was necessary. I did what anyone would've done. I was surprised when she asked if we wanted to have our fortune read. Before either of us had a chance to answer she took our left hands, the ones that link to the heart, she said.

A look of surprise crossed her elderly face. "You are a very special young lady. Your life is crossed with great happiness and great tragedy. You are selfless and giving. People will take advantage of that. No matter. Be true to your nature. It will serve you well. This young man—" She gave Duncan a sad look."You were not supposed to be together for some reason. It is a blessing to you both that you are. You will bring him the peace he seeks with desperation. He will save your life, more than your life." She went quiet, still. Duncan and I looked at each other, thinking she was finished.

"Be careful." She continued, looking at me. "One who loves you is trying to protect you. She is hurting. Bad people, beings that live in darkness, are looking for you. They want something from you and are willing to maim, torture and worse to get it. Beware of the man with blue eyes and a black star. His heart is turned." She trembled so much I thought she might fall apart. With difficulty I led her to a chair. She accepted my hand but wouldn't allow Duncan to touch her. "Now you must go. You have not much time. It was an honor to meet you **Unelmoija**."

We left the shop unsettled by her words. I meant to ask Duncan what the unel word meant but got distracted by a funny sign announcing cheap bathing suits and towels on the street as we were walking. To lift our mood we decided a swim was in order. We bought bathing suits and towels at a nearby store and went in the water. It was Duncan's idea. After the ominous predictions of the psychic we were eager to do something fun. I'd wanted to go to the beach ever since before Mom when out of town so I responded with an enthusiastic thumbs up. The water was warm. It was so calm and clear I could see the bottom. We hung out in the ocean, then half napped on the hot sand, sharing a companionable silence. I didn't want to spoil the moment by discussing bad things. Maybe we were both thinking about what the psychic had said.

We were walking back to the street from the beach when Duncan made a sudden movement and pulled me into a tight hug. All I saw was a blur before noticing we were blocks away in a quiet street between two tall buildings.

He stepped away from me and I saw blood on his shirt. "What happened?" I managed. "I'll call for help." His firm hand on mine and look of alarm stopped me in my tracks. "Uh... not a … good idea. Give me … a … moment." He leaned against the wall and closed his eyes. He was pale.

The buzzing not pleasant rhythm had changed. It seemed slower. I was afraid for Duncan and not sure what to do. I was wondering what had happened and trying to decide what to do when he spoke, his voice hoarse with pain.

"Bullet … in … shoulder. I reached toward him and he grasped my hands before I touched his shoulder. Wait. It's hot." I wasn't sure I understood what he meant. Was he saying his shoulder was hot? I touched it only to jerk my hand back from his burning shoulder.

A short time later he straightened and looked around the street. It was quiet. I'd only seen one person at the other end of the street since we arrived and she'd been busy talking on her cell phone, paying no attention to us.

Chapter 3

"Food. I need food." Duncan said with urgency.

"What a surprise." I tried for lighthearted and got a weak smile from him. "I'll walk to the corner to see what I find. Do you have money?" He nodded yes and reached for his wallet. I took a $20 bill and headed away from him."I'll find a place where we can sit together. I'm hungry too you know. It's been so long since we had anything to eat." That earned me another weak smile.

Minutes later I returned triumphant with a bag of fast food burgers, fries and a vanilla shake. As soon as he wolfed them down he looked more like himself. Food was more than energy for Duncan, I realized. It was his magic elixir, his cure all.

"I'm afraid you're stuck with me for dinner. Do you think you can survive another meal with me today?" Although he tried to put on a good face I could see he was still in pain, recovering from the bullet.

"You're lucky I'm hungry, buster. Unless you're up for a trek we have two choices within a short walk; the burger joint for another dose of fast food or a hoity-toity hotel." We walked arm in arm, allowing Duncan to lean on me for support without anyone noticing when we reached the busier street. He didn't lean much, probably afraid to put too much weight on me.

"Hoity-toity hotel wins. I'll get a room and we'll order room service. It's the safest alternative. It'll take time for me to heal." He glanced at me to make sure I was okay with the idea. "You don't look so good kiddo. Are you hurt?"

I was afraid for Duncan. He still looked pale and unsteady on his feet. I had a feeling Duncan never looked unsteady, ever. "I don't think so." I'd been so concerned about him it hadn't occurred to me that I might have been hit. I felt fine and saw no blood so I must be okay.

Check-in didn't take long. His black credit card got instant recognition from the woman behind the front desk. She called her boss, the duty manager, who informed us he was including a complimentary room upgrade and a bottle of champagne. "You can have the room for as long as you need it Mr. Bittersdorp. Let us know when you decide how long you want to stay and if there's anything you need, anything at all, at any time, don't hesitate to call me on my direct number." He handed Duncan his card. I reached for it and put it in his pocket.

I stood close to Duncan so they wouldn't notice the blood stain on his shirt. If they were surprised that we had no luggage the desk staff didn't let on. Within minutes we were in a large and luxurious waterfront room. Duncan plopped on the sofa. I made him lift his legs onto it.

"What should I do? What do you need? Water, food, a shot of bourbon?"

"I need food; a salad, no, two big salads and a steak with fries."

An hour after he ate Duncan fell asleep. It was a restless sleep, changing the rhythm of the not pleasant buzzing yet again. It seemed to do him good. I touched his forehead and it was so hot I was startled. I didn't know what was normal for someone like Duncan. I sat on the other sofa, watching him in case he needed anything. Now that things had calmed down I realized I was cold, so cold I was uncomfortable. A hot bath helped me regain some heat. I ate part of a leftover salad and sat back down near Duncan. He had saved my life at the beach like the psychic had predicted.

I must have fallen asleep because the next thing I knew a husky voice was teasing me about snoring. I didn't snore, I explained but it insisted I was snoring. I was happy keeping my eyes closed but the familiar husky voice was merciless.

"Who is it? Who are you?"

"Huh? I'm me, Duncan. Remember? We met today or was it yesterday? Had breakfast, lunch, and dinner, and oh yeah I took a bullet for you and saved your life after we went for a swim on the beach. Does any of this ring a bell?"

I opened my eyes, relief filling me, and looked at him, then around the room to make sure everything was the way I remembered it before falling asleep. I smelled the sea. It wasn't me because I'd taken a bath. The door to the balcony was ajar, allowing me to hear the surf and smell the ocean. A light breeze filtered into the dim lit room. It was quiet.

Perplexed I turned to him, "Why did you wake me you—you bully?"

"I didn't wake you so much as make sure you were awake. You were making odd sounds as if having a heated conversation. It didn't look like you were talking in your sleep. You didn't seem to be having a good time. Gallant man that I am, I intervened."

I realized he must be feeling better. He looked and sounded more like the old Duncan. I got a whiff of unwashed body which must be from him since I was clean. As if he'd read my mind he said, "I was about to jump in the shower when you started up with the animated conversating. I wanted to make sure you were alright. Did you check to see that the bullet didn't hit you?" I'd forgotten all about it. A quick examination proved I had a small gash where the bullet had grazed by me. It had scabbed over rather well.

After he showered I asked, "How are you feeling?" He was putting on a brave face but I wasn't sure he was completely healed. He still looked green around the edges, tired.

"Like a million bucks." I made a face. "Okay, maybe more like a thousand bucks. The good news is that I'll be fine with another few meals and some rest, and that we both survived the attack mostly unscathed. I'll order us some room service. We can discuss the situation while the food gets here."

How do you say thank you to someone when they save your life? I wasn't sure. Instead I asked, "How did you know about the shot? How did you know we had been shot at?"

He thought for a moment. "My ability to speed walk also gives me very fast reflexes, although my intention was to move you out of the way, not to get hit myself. The curious thing is that I never had a strong healing ability before. Like any healthy person, minor cuts and scratches heal quickly, but I felt something extraordinary after that injury. The bullet went through my body. It felt like I was boiling inside, but it hurt in a good way and the wound is nearly gone already."

"So you have the ability of super fast healing?"

"I never did before, but that's not the question you should be asking yourself right now."

"Ok, so what question should I be asking?"

"Who just tried to assassinate you with a large caliber bullet?"

.

Chapter 4

"I saw that shot coming from a third story window. It was a kill hot, aimed at your heart. If I hadn't been there it would have hit its mark. It was a professional shot and it was not going to miss. Yes, before you ask. My abilities are that good. I'm not saying that to boast, just so you understand the seriousness of the situation." He paused for a second to let me absorb what he said. The tough guy I had seen when we first met was back.

"That's why I didn't want to call for help. Then there are pesky police and things get complicated. I heard the shot coming toward you. The shot was meant for you." He stopped for effect.

It was then that we both realized how close to dying we had been. If he'd been an instant slower the bullet might have hit its mark or he could've died in my place. A shiver ran through me.

"Has someone tried to kill you before?" He tried for funny but I was too shocked and he was wary.

"Not lately. Okay, not ever that I know of. I don't suppose you saw who pulled the trigger?"

"Not really, I just heard the bullet."

"I wonder how the shooter found us. Even we didn't know we would be at the beach. It was a spur of the moment kind of thing. And, you're sure the bullet was meant for me, not you? Has someone tried to kill you before?"

He laughed. "I've been threatened plenty of times. They've even come close but this shot was aimed at you. I'm almost sure."

"Why would anyone want to kill me? I don't even know—" I caught myself before I revealed to Duncan how new I was to this whole abilities gig. I liked Duncan but Mom had taught me to play my cards close and someone had just tried to kill me while I was with Duncan. Only two people knew where we were and I hadn't told anyone where I was. As I was thinking that, it occurred to me that my father had given me a cell phone. I was pretty sure there was a way to track someone with a cell phone GPS signal.

Duncan was distracted pacing up and down the room like a caged cat. "Although several people know I came to Miami following McKnight no one knows my exact whereabouts. In case you're wondering if I ratted on you I haven't called or texted anyone all day. We've been together since early morning. I suppose you could think I had a chance to call or text someone while you or I went to the bathroom at some point. I didn't. Here, check my cell phone. I insist." He handed me his phone and I checked it while he watched me, resuming the pacing when I was done.

"What about you?"

"Yeah, that's it. I called someone to come and kill me. I scheduled it for when we returned from the beach."

"I meant do you have a cell phone? Someone could be tracking you with your phone."

I went to pull out the two phones I'd been carrying with me since the previous morning only to discover the phone my father had given me was missing.

I had Duncan check my phone for calls or text messages. That way we could trust each other again. The one Mom gave me was an old model with limited range and capabilities. Although I didn't have it with me I remembered that the other phone, the one my father game me, was modern and sleek.

"Mr. McKnight gave me a phone this morning. I had it with me all day." He stopped pacing and looked at me, surprise registering on his face.

"Could someone track our movements with our phones?" I knew Mom would never endanger my life. I didn't want to believe my father who I'd just met would be capable and willing to have me killed. I hoped the answer was a big fat no.

"Certain phones emit signals that allow tracking. When was the last time you remember seeing the phone?"

"When I set down my things at the beach before we went swimming."

He thought for a moment. "Someone could've taken it while we were swimming but I kept an eye on our things and didn't see anyone go near them." He was quiet again before speaking. "It's possible that if you had that phone with you all day that it led the killer to us." I felt like someone had punched me hard in the gut. My own father had tracked me then ordered a murder for hire.

"Why did he give you the phone?"

"So we could communicate. I … I can't believe it was him." I was torn between anger and pain. Tears streamed down my cheeks.

"Why would you need to communicate with him Amy? He's a dangerous, selfish bastard." I noticed he called me Amy instead of Just Amy when he was concerned.

"He wanted to get together again." My voice got small. Hearing it out loud, it sounded lame to me. Yesterday, when my father said it, it made perfect sense. I thought it was considerate of him to offer me a phone rather than to ask for my phone number. What kind of a man kills his own teenage daughter? How could he? Why would he?

"I don't understand. Together for what? What does that old bull want with someone like you?" I said nothing, hanging my head low, feeling sorry for myself, still not wanting to tell Duncan more than I had to about my relationship with my father. He went on wondering out loud. "And, he became protective when he saw me. Now that I think of it he wasn't offensive, didn't try to fight with me, he took a classic defensive stance blocking me from seeing you or approaching you. He shooed me away. You mean something to him. He was protecting you." He looked up at me for confirmation. I shrugged.

"If that was true he wouldn't have sent someone to kill me yesterday. That's the theory that makes the most sense."

"Let's think this through one step at a time. McKnight or another person who had knowledge of the phone, tracked you and sent a shooter to kill you. We don't know for sure that it was him, just that it was the phone he gave you that was probably involved in the tracking. It makes sense. There hasn't been a second attack because you lost the phone somewhere between the beach and here. A good thing too or we might both be dead."

"That theory makes sense." I said, feeling better at the thought that maybe it wasn't my father after all. If he didn't send the killer, it was possible the killer hurt my father to get the information. It wasn't that I liked my father. I didn't know him and the impression he'd made so far was, well, not impressive. Still, I wanted to believe that he didn't want me dead. I wished Mom was with me to help me figure out what was going on and answer the many questions that were swirling around in my head. At the moment, Duncan was my ally. He'd had ample opportunities to kill me since we met and instead he'd taken a bullet and saved my life.

"Besides, it makes no sense for him to hire a killer. He could've killed you with little effort yesterday. Instead, he protected you when I arrived."

"Hey Just Amy, don't worry. We'll figure this out. I'll help you. You haven't said anything much about your parents other than to mention your mother is out of town. I guessed you're on your own until she gets back. I know you don't know if you can trust me and we only met yesterday. Think about what you do know. We have been together almost every moment since yesterday morning. If I wanted to hurt you I could've done it at any time while we were together.

I'm not that kind of guy anyway but you don't know that. You can't go back to where you live until you know you're safe. The killer may know where you live. What can you tell me that might help us?"

"Believe it or not, I don't know much about what's going on. I've no clue why anyone would want to kill me. In my short life I haven't accumulated that many people who don't like me never mind want to kill me." I thought of Sara. She knew that I knew that she had killed her mother. Would she kill me if she had the chance? You betcha. Would she use sophisticated technology gotten through my father to do it? That was less likely though it was worth checking it out. "Mom and I were renting a small cottage from an older lady. Mom had to go out of town to take care of some important issues and left me there less than a week ago." It was hard to imagine so many things had happened to our quiet lives in the last three weeks. If it wasn't because of the danger it had been quite an adventure.

"A couple of days after Mom left, Sara, the woman's daughter who she seldom talked with announced she was coming to visit her. She made it clear she wasn't happy we were there. Soon after she arrived her mother died. At first the police thought it had been of natural causes but later they discovered she'd been poisoned and began to suspect Sara." I told him the rest of the story, leaving out the part about dreamshifting. "I can't imagine she was the one who tried to kill me yesterday."

"It doesn't seem like she was. What about McKnight? What does he want with you?"

"I don't know. Not for sure. Promise you will keep the next thing I tell you to yourself." He nodded his head up and down. "Pinky swear?" He gave me a strange look and then handed his pinky over. "He said he's my father." Duncan might've laughed. He remained serious, making me thankful that he believed me.

"What do you think?"

"I don't know why but I believe him. He said he wants to get to know me. I'm sure there's something else he wants. I don't trust him but I have a hard time believing he wants me dead." I must have looked a sad sight because Duncan reached over and hugged me.

Chapter 5

Feeling better after a few moments of human contact I agreed with Duncan that we should rest for the time being and look for answers after the sun came out. Taking the sofa for himself he gave me the bed. I was dog tired and fell asleep. It was a restful, deep slumber. When I woke up to the smell of bacon and eggs I saw Duncan reading the paper and making his way through his second plate of a hearty breakfast. Yawning I walked over to discover a covered plate filled with hot food for me. There was also juice, coffee and a fruit salad. I went for the fruit salad first. A hot ocean breeze was coming through the part open sliding glass door of the balcony. It was later than I expected, almost 11 a.m. I felt better having slept and Duncan looked like a new man; with sleep and breakfast he was going a long way toward recovery.

"Just Amy, I know you're not sure what you can tell me or how far you can trust me. For now we're in this together. I'll do whatever I can to protect you. You might think most people would walk away. I'm not most people. I've given this a lot of thought. I woke up before you did." He smiled. "When I've been in trouble I always had my dad or a family member to help me. You're all alone and too young to be facing a murder for hire by yourself. I'm not going to let them kill you, not if I can prevent it. Understand?"

Fear over my situation began to flood me when he said all alone. He was right. Mom wasn't here. I couldn't trust the man that had appeared in my life claiming to be my father a day earlier and I didn't know how to reach my sister, the only other person I'd have reached out to for support. "Yes. I— I— thanks."

"Let's see what we can figure out between us. First of all,

is there any way you can reach your mother? Will she call or did she leave you a phone number so you can call her?"

"Yes, I have her number in case of emergency."

"Someone almost killed you and shot me by mistake yesterday. I'm pretty sure that qualifies as an emergency."

I called Mom and left a short voicemail. It no longer mattered if someone was listening to our conversation. There was no point in trying to stay below the electronic surveillance cloud. The killer already knew I was in Miami. While we waited for her to call back we decided it was best if I stayed at the hotel while Duncan went to buy some clothes for us. We didn't think anyone knew we were there and it would be safer for him to go than to have me walking around South Beach with a killer looking for me.

Mom called back while Duncan was out. She didn't sound so good and I was making things worse for her with this call.

"Are you okay?"

"A little shook up. If it hadn't been for this guy I told you about I'd be dead now."

"I'm so sorry Ames. I thought you would be safer in Miami than with me. This has, as I expected, been a rough trip. I never dreamt they would try to have you killed."

"Who wants to kill me? Is it my father? I met him yesterday." She didn't seem surprised when I mentioned my father had found me. I wanted to ask her why she'd never said anything about him being free. Instead I let her answer my question.

"That's one of the reasons I said to be careful, not to use your— new skills. I was afraid he'd find you. I don't think he'd hire someone to have you killed after taking the trouble to figure out where you are and trying to make nice with you. He has plans for you. He would rather sweet talk you and win your graces to get what he wants. Besides, he has more to lose by your death than by your being alive. Someone close to him or someone tracking his moves found you. We need to make sure that doesn't happen again. I'll be in Miami in a little while and we can talk and decide what to do. Until then it's best if you are away from him. Can you stay where you are honey?" Mom only ever called me honey when she was worried.

I reassured her I was safe and we spoke for a few minutes longer. We agreed to meet three hours later. When Duncan returned I shared the good news. We would go together, we decided, after I explained what Mom had said.

He had news of his own. "I retraced our steps and found the phone your father gave you." I became alarmed thinking he had it with him.

"You didn't bring with you, did you?"

"You should know better. Well, I guess we've only known each other a short time. I was careful, paying a boy to pick up the phone and drop it off near some benches a long distance from the hotel. I waited a while and then picked up the phone and spent a few minutes looking at it. When I finished I pulled out the battery and tossed everything into the garbage. Although there were no missed calls or messages, your father texted you." To make sure he had it right Duncan wrote down the exact message: "Took care of CG problem. Person will never threaten you again. Token my affection."

"Your father has a reputation for not doing anything without a reason and a benefit for him. When he does it's serious. Did you ask him to help you with your problem? Do you know what problem and who he's talking about?" Duncan looked at me, his face serious and concerned.

The only CG problem I could think of was Sara. She, and her false report to the police, was the reason I had to move to Brickell. I wasn't sure what he meant by "took care."

"It's the story I told you already: Before moving to Brickell my mother and I'd been living in Coral Gables, a pretty area of Miami, renting a small cottage from a nice lady. While my mother was traveling the lady died. Right after her mother died Sara, that woman, told me to leave or she'd accuse me of stealing from her. Before I had a chance to leave she accused me anyway. It was thanks to the help of a near stranger that I was able to find a new place before things got worse. What's odd is I never mentioned any of that to my father and we didn't talk about it. I don't know how he found out. What do you suppose he meant when he said he took care of the problem?"

"If I had to guess I'd say she's dead." That was what I'd feared. Until he said the words it was just me thinking the worst.

"I'd hoped he'd paid her off, or scared her into leaving me alone."

"I doubt it. His solutions tend to be permanent. That was why I was concerned for you before you explained he was your father. We can check the newspaper for news about her."

Sure enough we found an article online. The police believed a gang had broken into her house. It was ransacked and burned. She'd been tortured before she was killed.

"What was the reason for this?" If he'd killed Sara it wasn't my fault. I knew that but somehow I felt a little happy inside that the woman might no longer be a threat to me, and that she'd paid for killing her mother. I felt relief and some amount of sadness. Did that make me just a little bit guilty? Should I feel bad?

"To impress you. To show you he cares by taking care of something for you. For him it was like sending flowers or a gift basket." Duncan's voice went up an octave. "And, he wouldn't like someone threatening and scaring his daughter. If word got out it would be a loss of face for him. How bad was it?"

"She was a drug addict and a nasty woman. She stole our rent money and forced me to move in a hurry because she accused me of stealing from her. If she could've hurt me more she would have." I didn't tell him the whole story because I'd have had to tell him about my dreamshifting. I felt bad about what had happened in the last dream as if somehow I could've handled things in a different way. I wondered for the umpteenth time if it had been necessary for me to break her arm. I knew the answer but I didn't like it.

"That was why he did it the way he did. It was a message. Mess with my daughter and you mess with me. In his own way he was protecting you, even if it was for selfish reasons."

"That doesn't make me feel better. I never asked for his help. What if I disagree with someone? Will he kill them too? What if I'm friends with someone he doesn't like or date someone he doesn't approve of will he do something to them?" I felt helpless, afraid and angry at the same time. Who did he think he was after so many years of never caring now he thought coming into my life and torturing and killing people on my behalf was his right as my father? That was part of the problem too. After so many years of wanting to meet my dad, a tiny part of me was happy to have a father who cared enough to kill Sara for me. Yes, that part liked the idea of a father who wanted to protect me. The rest of me thought killing, even a bad person like Sara, was wrong. "And, what will happen if I disagree with him one day? Will he use his ability on me?"

"Uncertain. Because of the similarity of their genetics, most children have a sort of immunity to their families' abilities. It's unpredictable and might backfire on them. And one of our oldest laws is that killing another Weeia is only condoned by a unanimous decision of all The Elders." Duncan said, trying to reassure me.

"And, killing Sara? Is that against the rules?"

"There the laws are fluid. If it's not necessary we're to refrain from killing others not of our kind, especially if it might bring unwanted attention. Since she threatened you and put you at risk The Elders would find in your father's favor. They might even applaud his efforts."

Soon it would be time to meet Mom and Duncan needed to eat. I was hungry too. We took full advantage of the room service menu, ordering more food than I thought we could eat. I was wrong. Although I surrendered early on, Duncan's appetite was quite up to the task.

Chapter 6

I was glad to see Mom. Even after hours of driving she looked good. She was a striking brunette in her late thirties, five foot three inches with a slender athletic build. Her short well-coiffed hair naturally matched her medium complexion and gray and brown magnetic eyes. The only sign the trip had taken a toll was an edge of tiredness in her eyes. As always she was well presented, wore a touch of makeup and clothes that suited her body type and coloring. We hugged. I cried (Mom's eyes were watery though she wouldn't admit it). I'd been so busy taking care of myself and trying to be an adult I hadn't realized how much I'd missed her. She wasn't just my mother she was my friend.

"Ames, quit worrying," she interrupted my thoughts. She knew me so well. "None of this is your fault. Some of it is mine for not telling you about this and preparing you much earlier. We'll talk later, okay?" I nodded my agreement.

"You must be the famous knight that saved my little girl's life," she reached out to hug Duncan, an unexpected and unusual gesture. Mom didn't like to touch strangers. Duncan hadn't said as much but I had the distinct impression he wasn't much into being touched by strangers either. Contrary to what I expected he hugged her back. We were inside a popular and crowded shopping center where Mom thought we would be safe for a short while.

"Your daughter is a charmer. Special too." He looked into her eyes for an answer.

"You have no idea," she laughed his question away. "I'm indebted to you Duncan. If in any way we can repay you, we're in your debt. Now we have to be going." She placed her hand on my shoulder to say we had to go and I should say my goodbyes. I hadn't realized we would be leaving

Duncan.

We had grown attached to each other in the last couple of days. It didn't cross my mind we would be going in separate directions. Now that she said it, it made sense. Duncan must have things to do and we had to figure out how to stay safe. I hoped we would see each other again. Before I could say anything Duncan spoke.

"Just Amy was great company. We have grown close in a short time. She … she's in danger and, with your permission, I want to help." I wanted his company and we needed someone on our side. Mom wasn't comfortable asking for assistance or accepting it. Neither was I. A little moral support was another thing.

"Mom, Duncan and I make a great team. Please say yes." She looked at me, surprised.

"This isn't only about you Ames. Helping us places him in harm's way. Your friend was nearly killed because he was with you." That made me sober up. I realized I was being selfish. Still, Duncan must have thought about the danger before offering. I hadn't asked. He'd volunteered.

"I'm aware that there's danger. I know of Amy's father's reputation and that he's a force to be reckoned with. You don't know me. I understand you have no reason to trust me. Trust my actions. If I'd wanted to harm Amy I could've done so in the last couple of days." This wasn't about trust. Or was it? I guessed there were more things Mom hadn't told me.

"You know there are other ways to harm a young woman," Mom responded without much force. We needed his support. She couldn't afford to turn down a friend. We didn't have that many.

In the end we agreed Duncan would work with us, at least until we found a way to keep me hidden and safe from whoever was trying to kill me. Figuring out who wanted me dead and why might take more time.

We decided against returning to the room I'd rented in the

Brickell District. There were too many unknowns. Besides, after my unexplained absence Rosario, the landlady, might have called the police to report me missing. I hoped they didn't think I had anything to do with Sara's death. I didn't want Officer Gomez, who had been kind to me when I needed it, to worry or be disappointed in me. I left her a voice mail message saying I was with my mother.

We still had the room at the hotel in South Beach. It had been safe for us so far and it was as good a place as any to spend the night until we found a solution. Whatever the manager thought when the three of us arrived he said nothing. Within minutes we had a second room that connected to our room. It was safer to be as close as possible we all agreed. The added room gave us extra sleeping space and a second bathroom. I liked being near the ocean, hearing the surf sounds and feeling the warm sea breeze. But for the danger there were nice things about our stay at the hotel.

When Duncan left a short while later to meet his contacts Mom and I had a chance to talk in private for the first time since she'd left Miami. I'd done my best to contain my fear and anger since she arrived. Now I wanted to know what was going on. She owed me answers and I was going to get them.

"I'm not quite sure where to start, Amy. Most Weeia have minor abilities that allow them to excel in a particular field, such as those who have superhuman tasting abilities and become famous chefs and wine experts; others who can see hundreds or thousands of colors, including infrared and ultraviolet, might chose a career in fashion design, paint development and related fields. A paranormal ability to smell may lead to a culinary path or one in perfume making. Some Weeia, like Duncan, have enhanced physical or mental abilities that allow them to succeed in the world of humans."

"What about you and my father?" I jumped in while she paused to continue the general introduction.

"Fair enough, let's talk about your father. When he was young, your father emerged as a powerful man among his peers. His particular mix of abilities was rare and useful, and he was being groomed to be a future Elder. I remember seeing him at parties and gatherings and knowing that he was going to be an important man. This was long before we had any romantic link. Something about the way he carried himself and his self confidence left me a bit in awe of him."

"Do you remember the Cold War between the United States and the Soviet Union?" The question caught me by surprise as I tried to remember those history lessons.

"Sort of, the Soviet Union was a communist country and they were working to spread communism to other parts in the world, and the United States wanted capitalism in those countries instead."

"During the early 1960s the missile crisis in Cuba had strained relations between the world powers. People feared an all out nuclear attack could happen at any time. Well, the fear of destruction was strong on both sides and a team of Weeia began working with the Soviet government, helping them to spy on the United States. A particularly strong Weeia, code named Red Death by the intelligence agencies in the United States, participated in multiple assassinations following the killing of President John F. Kennedy in 1963. It seems he could teleport himself to anyplace in the world, an ability on par with your father's ability to dreamshift."

"I had no idea this went back to such ancient history."

"Be careful young lady, I still remember those times myself."

"Sorry Mom." I lowered my voice, hoping there was enough contrition so that she'd continue the story.

"After the assassinations, the United States intelligence agencies dedicated most of their efforts to finding out how the Red Death operated and developing their own counter force. Eventually, either through informants or some other means, they approached your father and two powerful friends, and asked them to take part in an ambitious and unethical program. They could not refuse. Their mission was to put a stop to the Red Death project and undo the assassinations."

"That would require them to alter time in the past, can they do that?"

"It's very dangerous to attempt and requires massive amounts of power. Something went horribly wrong with the plan. Most of the assassinations were undone, but an entire city with tens of thousands of people disappeared from the face of the earth. Apparently only those who altered the timeline remember things before they were changed. That's why no one has any memory of the existence of New Lyon." That sounded so unbelievable. I was working hard to keep an open mind.

"Following the failure of the project your father somehow escaped. He became obsessed with the idea of repairing what they had done and reversing the loss, restoring the timeline to its previous state. The problem was that something like that had never been accomplished in the history of our people. No one knows if it's even possible." The more I heard the harder it was to get my arms around the concepts. This whole Weeia race came with some pretty incredible stories. Maybe it was a good thing that my mother waited until I was old enough to understand and grasp the complexities of being Weeia.

"I was unaware of most of this when I met him at another gathering. I still saw the dashing young man with the promising future and shortly after that we were married and happy for some time. First Kat, and then you were born. I thought you both would grow up in a normal household, healthy, happy and safe. Unfortunately, in time I discovered that your father planned to farm your abilities as soon as they manifested. In spite of the danger, he wanted to use our combined power to try to undo the damage he caused all those years ago." Mom had a funny look on her face. I guessed she was traveling back in time. It must've been a shock for her to discover her husband's plans for his family were not the mundane and benign life she had dreamed of when they married. I felt for her. It must've been a sad and scary time in her marriage.

"I think the repeated use of his abilities warped your father's personality, converting a happy, loving and caring man into a grumpy, selfish power hungry being. The guilt of all the loss of life from the destruction of New Lyon was eating him from the inside," Mom said, deep sadness straining her features. "He convinced himself that his ability combined with mine and that of our two children would be enough to restore the past. When it became apparent that he'd sacrifice himself, and his entire family to attempt to clean up the disaster, I made a plan to get you girls out of his reach. I couldn't allow him to risk our safety and well being even if it had been a sure thing. Risking so much on an unproven theory was just crazy." I stayed quiet, wanting to hear the story of my parents breakup for the first time. All those years growing up, I had not questioned my mother's story much. I didn't think Kat had either.

"By this time, he was working as the enforcer for The Elders, a role that earned him many enemies. He also started working with the United States government, for the CIA, doing counter-espionage and helping The Elders prevent a repeat of the Cold War mistakes. I convinced your father that if he kept doing such dangerous work and making enemies, eventually we would all become targets. He wouldn't accept that we were in danger, but the stage was set. I created a powerful illusion that we'd all been killed in a massive accident, fooling everyone including your father." She paused with a look of relief on her face, keeping things bottled up for all those years had taken its toll on her.

"You know most of the rest. We lived off the grid, and I avoided any use of my own abilities to hide us from the Weeia, including your father. To keep you safe I kept silent until, if and when, either of you showed abilities. This meant isolating all of us from our people, culture and identity, a sacrifice I was willing to make."

I began to suspect this had been hardest on her. "It must have been difficult having your family think we were all dead."

"The real problems started when your abilities surfaced early without you knowing what they were. Since you didn't know there was anything special about what you were experiencing you didn't say anything to me. It isn't clear what abilities Kat might have or if it was just the emergence of your ability that made it possible for your father and the kidnappers to find us. I'm very worried about Kat; she seems to have disappeared without a trace."

We didn't discuss my ability. It was like the big elephant in the room nobody talked about. Mom had explained people kept their abilities secret. Knowing a person's abilities made them vulnerable to attack. Some of the anger I felt toward my mother faded away.

"I understand that you did the best you could. It's been hard for us and now I see it was a decision you were forced to make to keep us safe from my father. It must've been hard on you too. What I don't understand is why my father is so interested in me or why anyone would want to kill me."

"Ames, honey it's more complicated than that." She paused for a moment and I felt myself bursting with questions. She looked at me and sighed "I know you want to know everything right now, but there's a great deal to talk about and we have little time. We need to get some rest tonight and once we're someplace safe, there will be time to discuss it all."

"Okay." I had so many questions.

"The important thing right now is that you tell me about your dreamshifting. Tell me everything you remember, even little things are important, since I left. Don't leave anything out." So I did. I described my dreams in detail even the parts I felt bad about.

"You have stronger power than most Weeia I've encountered. Even without using your ability I can feel it. That's why you're able to spend time with Duncan even though you're opposites and being together should bother you. For some opposites being with another opposite is painful. Your power is so strong it allows you to overcome the batjar. I think that's why you're able to go with him on his walks when others can't. Also, I believe one of the Weeia gifts you have inherited is to make other people feel happy around you and comfortable. It's a rare gift. That's part of the reason, in addition to your natural charm, why he feels comfortable around you even in spite of the batjar."

"So he likes my ability, not me?" I was confused.

"Not precisely. This is a lot to absorb in a short amount of time. I know. I'm so sorry Ames. I should've said something sooner to prepare you. I thought keeping quiet was the best way to protect you until we knew for sure if you had abilities. Many Weeia never develop abilities or develop weak ones. I wish we had time for you to deal with all of this but your life is in danger. Someone wants to kill you. We need to find out who it is and the reason they want you dead. That'll be the best way to keep you out of harm's way. We're going to have to hide until your abilities strengthen, and you learn how to use them and hide them. We need all the help we can get right now."

Duncan was well connected and willing to ask for shelter on our behalf. All my life I had learned to stand on my own, relying only on Mom and Kat for support as a last resort. We never asked anyone else for aid. Accepting Duncan's friendship had been easy. Welcoming his help had been difficult. Agreeing to let him ask others to assist us now went against everything I knew. I was sure Mom would agree with me when I turned down his offer to find a place for us to live. Instead she said she'd be grateful. Who was this woman and what had she done to my mother?

"That's why you accepted Duncan's offer?"

"Yes, Ames. So far he has proven he's your friend and that we can trust him. He kept you safe even when he knew who your father was. He could've turned you in, he could've killed you, or he could've sold you out to our enemies." Our enemies? How many were there, I wondered. Mom was right; I had a lot to learn. I knew she was worried. Our situation was difficult to say the least. Feeling there was a target on my back and being trapped indoors was making it harder to cope.

Duncan returned a couple of hours later looking pleased. "A family who is acquainted with my family has offered you refuge here in Miami, no strings attached. I don't know them well myself though I know of them. Your father has made many enemies and this family is politically opposed to his agenda. They were more than willing to provide a safe place within their guarded compound for someone he might be tracking." Making an exaggerated gesture to indicate suffering he said, "I'm starving again; do you want anything from room service?"

Mom pulled me aside while Duncan called down for some food. "A well guarded compound cuts both ways. We'll be protected from outsiders. At the same time we could become their prisoners."

Duncan returned from the other room. "The good news is that you'll be together, and they have staff onsite that can train you Amy. That way you can learn to use your abilities and shield yourself from other Weeia. If the assassin doesn't know where you are he or she can't shoot you."

"It makes sense. I like the 'can't shoot' me part. Do you

think it might be a woman?"

"It's not probable but it's possible. There are Weeia with abilities ideal for such work. The plan is to meet up with them in a parking garage to make sure we're not being tailed. From there we'll follow their vehicle to the property. After that, I have to head back west to take care of some business matters, but I'll be able to visit you regularly." He looked a touch sad.

No solution was ever perfect. For the time being this option solved our immediate problems. If we got into trouble later I'd be stronger and better able to manage my abilities than I was before, and if she had to, maybe Mom would use hers since we wouldn't have to worry about hiding from my father.

Chapter 7

After a restful night we had breakfast in our rooms. I'd never seen so much breakfast food in one place that was not a restaurant. There were eggs in two styles, scrambled and Benedict; salmon and cream cheese on a bagel; sides of corned beef hash, breakfast sausages, Canadian peameal bacon and crispy bacon; granola French toast and fluffy pancakes with maple syrup; fresh fruit, and yogurt. Between the three of us almost everything disappeared.

Although there was a lot of nervous energy in the air I felt better knowing Mom was back in one piece, and we had a safe haven to go to for a while. I was a little sad thinking I'd miss Duncan. Even though we'd only known each other for a couple of days, I enjoyed his company. A lot of things happened during our time together. I was grateful to him for saving my life and finding a place for us to live out of harm's way. To lift my mood I decided on a direct approach.

"Why so serious Speedy?"

"I'm not serious as much as sleepy." I was not buying that for a minute.

"Sleepy? How can you be sleepy and consume enough breakfast sides for a battalion? I think you're worried you're going to miss me. Who's gonna show you around Miami after today? Who's gonna speed walk with you?" That had been too close to the mark and I regretted saying it as soon as the words escaped my lips.

"Ames, leave the young man in peace to enjoy the last of his meal and the beach view." My mother sounded amused. I think she was surprised at how well Duncan and I got along. It was unusual for her to warm up to someone she'd just met the way she seemed to have done with Duncan.

"Fine. If I can't pick on Duncan then I'm going for a swim

before the pool gets crowded."

"No." Their two voices replied in near unison.

"Touchy, touchy. A girl's gotta try." I smiled. I'd been sure I wouldn't get away with a swim even if the pool was empty, in light of the attempt on my life. I still had the bathing suit and it might be the last chance I had to go swimming in a while. Either way, it was worth trying just to see the looks on their faces.

"Let's go over the plans for today." Mom, dressed in khaki pants, a white top and matching white canvas shoes, encouraged a return to reality.

"A staff member gave me clear instructions. We'll drive to the rooftop of the shopping center parking garage in Coconut Grove. I know the place. They'll meet us there and make sure no one is tailing us. From there, we'll follow them to Douglas Estate where you'll settle in the lap of luxury until next we see each other."

"Lap of luxury?"

"Is it a luxury property?" Mom asked, sounding surprised.

"I don't know but it sounded good, didn't it? The name is Douglas Estate so I assume it's big. The family is wealthy and has properties in several countries. They don't live here and spend little time in Miami. As far as I know, they only use this property for retreats. I assume it'll be comfortable at least."

"All I care about at this point is that it be safe."

"The person I spoke with assured me it is."

"Mom, I don't have many clothes. Everything I have is still at the apartment in Brickell. I like your new pants, by the way. Can we stop and pick up a few things for me on the way?"

"No." In stereo again.

"Once we're settled in you can get some clothes. I'd rather not be out in the open any more than we need to. You can go to the hotel gift shop if you like."

"Okay." I brightened. Maybe they would have a cute t-shirt or summer pants to replace my current uncomfortable attire.

My gift shop excursion netted little in the way of clothing although I made good use of the time by buying some snacks. A couple of hours later we left the hotel toward Coconut Grove. It was not far but the traffic in Miami was unpredictable and we didn't want to be late. We arrived with time to spare. There were only a handful of cars in the garage rooftop. We found a parking space in the middle next to a plain brown coupe. Duncan took a close look to see if it belonged to the people we were there to meet.

"It's empty. I didn't think it looked right to be their car but I just wanted to double check."

Ten minutes later a black limo appeared. While Mom kept our car running, Duncan walked to the driver's side to introduce himself and get any last minute instructions. He returned saying they wanted to meet us before heading out. My nervous energy was getting the better of me. I needed to walk, jump, do something. I got out of the car. As she moved to open the door Mom dropped her handbag onto the floor of the car and some of the contents spilled. I guess I wasn't the only one with nervous energy to spare.

"Amy, wait a sec. Your mother needs to sort herself out." Duncan stayed behind helping Mom gather something that had fallen under the seat while I stood next to the car hopping from foot to foot.

"It's okay Amy. I just need a minute. Go on ahead if you just want to say hello. We'll be there in a jiffy."

As I was nearing the limo, I heard a massive sound and a powerful blast pushed me forward towards the car. After that, there was a lot of confusion. Without realizing it, I'd fallen to the ground. Thick, acrid smoke filled the air. It hurt to breathe and my eyes stung. I couldn't see Mom or Duncan. I wasn't sure where our car was or the limo. There was an eerie silence. I couldn't hear anything. As I began to get up I felt strong arms lift me and carry me into the limo. There was no one else.

"Where's Mom? I'm not leaving without my mother." I tried for a scream. My throat was sore but I tried anyway. I couldn't hear myself or anything else. It was like someone had stuck cotton in my ears. There was still smoke in the rooftop. I looked for Mom and Duncan as we drove away. Seeing nothing I spoke again. There was no one to answer. I tried to open the doors. They were locked. I pounded on the limo's partition the whole way to Douglas Estate.

I was still wobbly when we arrived. A tall man in a business suit lifted me like I was a rag doll. He set me down in a cushioned seat in a living area and walked out. My eyes still stung, my throat hurt and I was unsteady on my feet. Worse of all the silence still enveloped me.

A couple of hours later, a young Asian woman brought me tea. Her clothes and shoes were worn and old. She looked shy and uncertain. She spoke no English. After I drank the tea I slept for several hours. When I woke it was dark, the middle of the night.

The following day the young woman returned with a simple meal. I ate it, frustrated we couldn't communicate. I asked her, in English and using my hands, about my mother and Duncan. She'd wave her hands back and forth saying, "no English, no English." She went on to say other things in a language I couldn't identify before leaving.

I was starting to feel anxious and thinking of walking out of the property when she returned. In her hand was an envelope with my name on it.

Dearest Amy,

The staff at Douglas Estate tell me you're safe. I was glad when I found out they took you away. There was no one else on the roof so we were the only ones left after the explosion. Duncan and I went to the emergency room. Duncan had some cuts and bruises which should heal soon. I just breathed too much smoke and had to sit down for a bit.

I have to take care of some important business and will be away for a while. Duncan has to return home for work. We'll be back as soon as we can.

For your own safety it's important that you stay at Douglas Estate. They will take good care of you. Whatever you do, don't try to follow me or visit Duncan. Just stay put until we return.

Love,

Mom

I thought Mom's handwriting looked a bit off; she was probably more shaken up than she liked to admit. At least she and Duncan were safe and I was too. I was glad to be in a place where I could learn more about my abilities and how to use them. I was too excited to sleep, but forced myself to lie down and relax; thinking the next day was going to be the beginning of an exciting new phase of my life.

Chapter 8

Douglas Estate, a waterfront residential compound, was tucked in the upscale part of Coconut Grove, a central neighborhood on the east side of Miami. Even by the standards of that area it was enormous. Most of the property was construction free. It had received historic landmark designation and protection from a national organization whose name I'd seen on a placard and forgotten. The buildings though old had been updated to include modern amenities like showers and toilets but no air conditioning.

The owners, who were not there when I arrived, lived somewhere else. A security staff hired from an outside company did shifts on the property, but didn't live there. As far as I knew, the only residents were three staff members. Zhao Tse, the man designated to train and guide me, appeared to be in charge. Ping, a grubby man with black cloth shoes, and Lala, a sad looking young woman who did whatever Ping ordered and I thought might be his daughter, were the other residents. Only Zhao, who told me to call him Master Tse, spoke English.

Ping and Lala showed me to my quarters. I was to live in a simple yet comfortable room in the main house, the sole occupant of that building. They lived in another building on the property where I was not supposed to go. I saw them twice a day. In the morning, they brought my meal of broth, rice and a fruit, and at night they brought me tea. They spoke an Asian language I couldn't understand. We communicated with hand signals when necessary. They showed little interest in communicating with me.

My days became routine. Every morning, I woke up before dawn, walked along a foot trail for one hour. Most days I visited the bayside Cabana where I waited for sunrise. It was a pretty trail and I enjoyed the walk, listening to nature's sounds such as the clicking and buzzing of insects, bird song and, as I approached the Cabana, the sounds of the surf. The Cabana had shade, some furniture, fresh water and little else. I liked it because it felt private, like my own corner of the large estate.

There, I spent several hours meditating before returning to the main house. By mid afternoon when I returned Ping or Lala brought my meal. Then there was a brief session with Master Tse and my time was free until Ping or Lala arrived with my bedtime tea.

When I arrived at the compound Master Tse was on his best behavior. That lasted for only a short time. Master Tse revealed himself as a hard task master. His style was one of deprivation. He lectured me on the ills of abusing my superhuman abilities and indulging in desires of the flesh, including overeating. The latter must have had more to do with his desires than mine, I thought amused when I considered his rotund midsection. Master Tse explained that use of my abilities was allowed only under his supervision. He'd know the minute I used my abilities and the penalty for disobedience was three days of isolation. The problem was that I didn't know how to start or stop my abilities. That was the reason I'd gone there in the first place.

I didn't mind the isolation. After all it was not like Ping, Lala or Master Tse were pleasant company. They were not much company at all. What bothered me was the hunger. He didn't mention my meager meals would also be withdrawn. In time, I found two solutions. First, I learned to use my abilities without his knowledge. Also, I discovered a trail to a neighboring property bursting with fruit trees. Although the grounds were well kept no one seemed to pick the fruit from the trees so I didn't feel I was harming anyone or taking fruit they might use. Eating the fruit helped with the hunger on those days when I wanted to practice my abilities in solitude. The rest of the time, they supplemented the meager amounts of food they gave me.

Not long after I arrived I started to get horrible debilitating headaches. They began as a mild general discomfort and grew until the pain and malaise were so severe all I wanted was to lie down in a dark and quiet place. My temples throbbed, my eyes hurt when they came in contact with light, and I had trouble thinking or focusing for long. I also lost my appetite and became listless. They lasted for a day or two sometimes even three days. During that time, dreamshifting was painful. I had noticed the tea made me feel tired, I started to believe that either the tea or food might be drugged.

One day, I dropped something in my room and when I bent down I noticed tiny red lights embedded into the wall just a few inches above the floor that hadn't been there before. The next time I became ill I noticed the lights blinking. I paid attention and found that every time I had a headache the lights would be blinking. When they stopped blinking my discomfort became milder and disappeared.

My dreamshifting ability had diminished since I arrived. When I mentioned it to Master Tse he appeared pleased and said that was for the best. When I asked about practicing my ability he'd find an excuse not to practice and remind me that practicing on my own was forbidden.

One night, as I looked down at Ping's feet while he handed me my bedtime tea I decided I'd escape. I remember that moment with perfect clarity. It's seared in my mind. He was wearing the same cloth black shoes he wore every day. They were so worn I could see the shape of his toes. The fabric was a faded shade of color somewhere between black and nothing with a proper name.

As he leaned down to give me the cup the clean scent of the night disappeared. The pungent smell of grease mixed with cooking odors that was his personal fragrance reached me like a physical thing as it had every night for weeks. The sallow skin of his hand punctuated with, what I assumed were, food stains, ended in dirty, torn and broken nails. Above his hand his grayish black sleeve had been pushed up allowing me to see the thick black hairs on his arm.

The evening was silent except for the sounds of nature in February in Miami. Florida's most populous southern city was a congested, sometimes ugly place. It extended north in one continuous urban area divided into many municipalities. To the west, it was bounded by the swamps of the Everglades and to the east, the Atlantic Ocean. Traffic filled up the arteries connecting the residential and commercial centers the better part of the daytime hours. While urban sounds might dominate most neighborhoods, the area where I was living temporarily was isolated. The part of the neighborhood I'd seen was made up of leafy narrow streets, with hedge hidden homes, that led to narrower shady streets lined with posh houses.

Although I kept my eyes down and my posture tired, my heart was hammering. It was so loud in my head I feared he could hear it. I made myself take deep, slow, deliberate breaths to calm down. When I felt my mind still, I imagined the tea cup to be already empty. A moment passed until I felt its weight shift in my hand. I made motions like I was drinking the foul liquid and set my head on the pillow. The decision had surprised me, springing into my head like a bolt of lightning. For the first time since I arrived at that place I knew what I had to do and I was confident I'd be successful. I wouldn't let anything get in the way.

Everything was different when I woke up. I realized I had a new perspective. My decision had changed me. I didn't yet know how I'd escape but I was sure that I would. In theory I could leave the compound anytime I wanted. While there was security to protect the property from outsiders I should be able to walk off the grounds without anyone stopping me. I'd never tried to do it in the open. I believed, based on my observations when walking around the estate, the guards wouldn't stop me from leaving.

In her letter, Mom had asked me to stay at the estate and I had nowhere to go if I left. I had no money, no friends and no family in Miami. Making my way without identification or money on the streets of Miami was risky. For me it could be worse. The killer might still be in the city or might be able to find me the same way he had before, if I left the safety of the compound.

Growing up with the fear of being kidnapped had forced me to be aware of my surroundings at all times and suspicious of everyone. Being kidnapped and then escaping had taught me that other than my mother the only person I could count on was myself. The stress of that experience had also triggered my superhuman abilities and made me grow up fast. It wasn't clear who was responsible for the attempts on my life. I could no longer worry about that problem; I needed to escape Douglas Estate.

When dreamshifting I could change things any way I wanted within the limits of my ability whatever they were. Why not dream myself out of this situation? Since I arrived at the compound my ability to dream had changed. Master Tse was supposed to teach me about my ability, what it was, how to control it, how to use it, how to hide it when I used it so others of my race wouldn't know where I was, the benefits, the dangers, the side effects and more so that I'd grow strong and independent, and with time leave the compound. Instead, my ability had grown weaker than before I arrived and I felt ill and tired all the time.

I wasn't sure why my mother and Duncan had never contacted me after I received that letter. During my tenure at Douglas Estate, the situation had steadily gotten worse. I was finished with the isolation and being lied to and poisoned. I didn't like feeling tired and ill much either. Nobody else was coming and it was up to me to escape that predicament. I was on my own again.

Every day I practiced daytime dreamshifting. I had the feeling Master Tse was keeping an eye on me so I was careful to make the dreamshifts about simple things that wouldn't draw his attention. In a short time, I could make small objects appear and move about with little effort. Master Tse almost caught me one day when I chuckled out loud while dropping tiny leaves into his hair for grins. I made them disappear quickly and stifled my laughter.

I also practiced reaching out with my senses during my daily meditation period. When he asked about the meditation I said it helped quiet my mind and ease the headaches. He seemed satisfied with the answer. After several days of not drinking the evening tea, my senses sharpened. I felt stronger, more lucid and with more energy. I had to work hard to fake the drowsiness that had engulfed me before.

On a day when Master Tse was out of the estate I took advantage of one of the meditation sessions to explore the state of restful half sleep I'd learned to find. I focused all my energy and will on locating Mom. To my surprise I found myself in a hospital room. I was in a dream like state and at the same time I was aware of my surroundings, my mental state and my physical location as I was when I meditated. I was dreamshifting while awake. My father had told me this was possible. A single occupant was on the bed tethered to monitors and intravenous cables. An antiseptic smell, and the whirring and beeping sounds of the machines confirmed I was in a medical facility.

I knew before I saw her face it was Mom. At first glance she appeared to be sleeping. I was so excited to see her I rushed to her bed. I knew Mom would have been with me if she could have. I told myself that the reason she'd been away was that she was still recovering from the wounds from the explosion and didn't want me to worry. Big fat tears of joy at finding Mom flowed down my cheeks. As I reached out to wake her I realized she was not asleep. Between all the medical jargon, I figured out from reading the medical chart that hung from her bed that she was in a coma. She'd been like this since the explosion that day in the Coconut Grove parking garage.

Chapter 9

I startled myself out of the meditation, still upset. My mother was in a coma and needed my help. That was proof Master Tse had been lying to me since my arrival. The note I received hadn't been from my mother because she'd been in the hospital for weeks. I had to do something. Someone had forged that letter from Mom to keep me cooped up in the property under Master Tse's thumb. At that moment, I understood I had to find a way to improve my skills so I could leave the property for good to aid Mom.

I didn't know how I'd do that. I'd figure it out along the way. In the meantime, I'd continue to practice dreamshifting on the sly and strengthen my abilities as best as I could. Whoever these people were they were powerful and they played for keeps. I didn't understand why they had welcomed us only to thwart my abilities. It was clear that to find my way out of the situation I needed help. I thought of Kat, my older sister. We had lost touch weeks before. Wherever she was I hoped she was safe. I wished I could reach her. We would be able to fight this together.

After Kat, I thought of my father. I knew little about him. We had only met a few days before I arrived at Douglas Estate. He had a strong personality and a strong will. The main reason I thought about him was that he was a powerful and dangerous man. Our relationship, what little we had, was complicated.

He'd appeared in my life out of nowhere soon after my abilities surfaced, introducing himself as if I hadn't spent my whole life without a father. I was unconvinced he had my or Mom's best interests in mind. I wondered if we were connected by a strong bond like he had told me. Anytime I used my powers he could feel it, he said. That was how he'd found me when no one from our race, not even Mom, knew my whereabouts.

All that was required for me to reach him, he'd said, was for me to wish it. Because we suspected the person who shot at me had found me with my father's phone I didn't dare contact him then. The main reason I'd gone to Douglas Estate was because the property was supposed to be protected from such bonds. Within the property, I was told, my father would be unable to sense me and the bond my father had said we shared would be blocked. I assumed it worked since I hadn't seen him. Then again, I'd kept my dreamshifting to a minimum.

When I had practiced my dreamshifting at Douglas Estate I had also practiced cloaking the dreams so other Weeia and my father wouldn't detect them. I didn't know for sure if it was working. So far Master Tse showed no indication of knowing about my dreamshifting and there had been no sign of my father. The last time, the only time, we had spoken we had agreed I would be in touch two days later. Because of the explosion and my move to the estate I never contacted him. He must've wondered what had happened. Perhaps he thought I decided I didn't want to talk to him again.

Now, I needed my father to make Mom better. I was sure he would have ideas and resources that could make a difference. I didn't know how he would respond if I reached out to him. If he was behind the attempt on my life he could kill me if I made contact. I had thought a lot about my father since that day. If he'd wanted to kill me it would have been easy for him. Why hire a gunman to shoot me when he could kill me with a mere thought? It made no sense. Why approach me and introduce himself, then send someone after me? I was so afraid I hadn't given him a chance to explain.

Now, what mattered was Mom. As long as I was bound to Douglas Estate for safety, she lingered in the hospital in a coma alone. I didn't need the doctors to tell me that the longer she was there the less likely it was that she'd come out of the coma unharmed. If my father could do something, I had to reach him even if by contacting him I risked my life.

So many things I thought about this place were incorrect. Perhaps that while I was at the estate my father's connection with me was blocked was one of them. When I thought it through it seemed silly. At the time I first heard about it the thought gave me hope and made me feel safe. Even if it was untrue contacting him from the estate would give away my location. That would leave me unprotected, exposed. I had to do it from another place. I couldn't get far enough from the compound on foot for it to matter. I needed to go back to Brickell Avenue in the central part of the city or somewhere else away from the estate. That was when I thought of Duncan. Since I arrived Duncan had never visited even though he'd promised to be in contact.

I hadn't seen Master Tse for several days. My growing worries about Mom emboldened me. I decided to explore the property while dreamshifting in search of information that would be useful in my efforts to leave and find a way to get my mother get out of her coma.

I remembered Mom's warning about dreamshifting with hesitation. I was sure she would understand that there were exceptions to every rule. It was clear to me this was one of those times. There was a risk that if Master Tse was at Douglas Estate he'd know when I had a dream. He had made it clear I was only to do that under his close supervision. To date, that had been never. On the other hand, I had tried it already and he hadn't said a word or even made an appearance. I believed he was somewhere else.

It was also possible that my father's bond would give my location away to him when I dreamshifted. I had no idea if the technique I'd been working on to keep my ability to myself worked. I'd half expected my father to show up on my doorstep after my first visit to Mom at the hospital. To my immense relief there had been no sign of him. Either he hadn't detected my dreamshifting or he had better things to do and was ignoring me. At that point no news was good news.

I decided to take the opportunity. In real life, unlike fairy tales, the princess had to fend for herself and find her own way. I couldn't afford to wait for prince charming, whoever he was, to rescue Mom. Tempus fugit, I remembered the Latin phrase from an action movie.

In my dream, I explored the next door building. I made sure to do it at a time when Lala and Ping would be out of the estate grocery shopping. As I expected, the building where they lived was different from mine. It appeared to be the staff quarters and featured no air conditioning or fans. While it was larger, as if for many more staff, the furnishings were simple and few.

The sleeping area was messy and the kitchen was downright filthy. Asian newspapers were strewn on the floor next to empty food containers, fruit peel, clothes, empty luggage, and discarded wrappers. There were odd plastic and paper bags in staggered sizes. I assumed they contained spices or herbal remedies. I saw several large cockroaches and there were ants crawling on top of the kitchen counter and around some of the food leavings. The owners must not have known about their lack of hygiene or didn't care. I supposed since they seldom visited the estate they knew little of what their staff did on site.

Just as I turned to leave in disgust I noticed stacks of currency, mostly twenty dollar bills, on a shelf in one of the few items of furniture. There were hundreds of thousands of dollars in bills of several denominations on several shelves, like rows of books stacked on top of, in front of and every which way. Once I escaped the open jail that was Douglas Estate I'd need money until my mother was back on her feet. She'd had most of the money we were bringing with her. The little I had left was in my handbag in the car when we were in the parking lot. After the explosion it stayed behind along with a handful of my belongings.

With a pang of guilt at taking someone else's money I removed two thousand dollars from the lowermost shelf hoping the owners or keepers wouldn't notice. Knowing how unkind they had been to me all those weeks, drugging me and showing not the slightest warmth toward me made it easier. When I dreamshifted my body stayed where it was and a part of me went into the dream. I wasn't sure if dreamshifting allowed me to transport solid things like money. I'd been able to rid myself of the nighttime tea so I was hopeful bringing something back would work too. I looked around the rest of the building before leaving. Nothing more caught my attention.

When I woke up from my dreamshifting the folded over money with a slight layer of grease was in my pocket. I could get used to this dreamshifting ability, I thought with a smile. No wonder my father liked it. It rocked, as Mom would say.

The next task on my list would be harder. I needed to get in touch with Duncan. He was the only person I trusted other than Kat and Mom. I hoped I'd be able to find him and that he'd be willing and able to help me.

Several times I'd dreamshifted with no bad results. Confident my blocking abilities were working I set out to find Duncan in my next dream. I wasn't sure where he was at that moment but I remembered he'd said he lived in Seattle, almost as far as he could be from where I was and still be within the mainland of the United States. I hoped with all my might that he'd be able to return to Miami.

After I appeared in his room it occurred to me I might have found him in a compromising position, in mixed company or somewhere he didn't want to be seen. As luck would have it, he was fast asleep. It was a large room with a striking view of the water. I tapped his shoulder to wake him up.

He turned over and peered at me with barely open eyes. "Wha, huh? What's going on?"

"Hi Fastman. Don't be alarmed. It's me, dreamshifting. I'm not sure how much of this will make sense or how it will appear to you. If you only remember one thing, remember this: I need your help. Please come to Miami as soon as you can. You'll find the address of Douglas Estate in a text on your phone." As I said the words I knew the text would be in Duncan's phone.

I had no phone for him to reply. Mine had been in my handbag in the car when the bomb exploded. Other than at the guardhouse I had seen no phones at my prison home. Three nights in a row I visited Duncan. My visits were short but they allowed me to make sure Duncan knew the dreams were real. I didn't dare linger for fear I would be found out.

It occurred to me that if he traveled all the way to where I was the guards wouldn't let him enter. I used other dreams to make my way to the guardhouse. Over several days, I watched as the guards let delivery and service staff enter the grounds. Every time someone arrived at the gate they checked a clipboard that hung from the air conditioned guardhouse desk. On the board there was a list of the people allowed access that day. All I had to do was think my wish that Duncan's name be there and it appeared on the list. I double checked to make sure. There it was in plain block letters identical to the other names on the list, "Duncan Bittersdorp." It was crazy how those two words could make me feel so much better.

As I turned to leave I noticed an unusual stone by the gate. The color didn't match the rest of the rocks on the ground. There was a soft glow to it that the others didn't have. Looking closer I found several others like it scattered at irregular distance from each other and only around the entrance area. Something about them made me uncomfortable when I tried to cross to the other side. I didn't like the feeling. I had never experienced anything like that.

I walked out in spite of the discomfort thinking the stones were designed to keep intruders out of the property. From the other side they looked the same but when I crossed the entrance in the opposite direction I felt no discomfort. It dawned on me that the stones weren't meant to keep anyone from coming in to the estate they were there to keep whoever was in from leaving. Since other than the staff I was the only resident whoever had placed the pebbles there wanted me locked within.

I didn't want the stones blocking my way when Duncan and I left to visit my mother or anytime I wanted to go out. My misgivings about Douglas Estate grew. Whoever was behind the stones was trying to keep me from leaving the property. Between this barrier, the tea and the lights I was a virtual prisoner as far as they knew. I concentrated on them for a few seconds and they disappeared.

I woke up feeling optimistic after a restful dreamless night. I feigned tiredness as I moved around in case one of the staff saw me. It had been ten days since I had last seen Master Tse. He left without a word to me. Ping and Lala of course couldn't or wouldn't speak English and there was no one else that might know or tell me if they did.

Every day and night since Master Tse left I practiced my skills, waiting for the right moment. I was about to head out on the walking trail in search of fruit and to my meditation place when I heard voices.

"Amy. Where are you? I know you're here somewhere," a familiar voice said.

My heart sped up at the sound of the voice. Before my brain had time to process what was happening, another part of me recognized the source and I moved in that direction.

"I'm here." I heard myself yell as if the words belonged to

someone else.

"Where's here? Keep talking and I'll follow the sound."

"I'm in the main building, the house." Duncan had made his way to Miami. Realizing main building meant nothing to him I told him to look for the building made of coral rock. While it was not the most modern it was the largest of the buildings within Douglas Estate, at least the ones I'd seen. I walked to the front of the house and continued speaking. Duncan had gone quiet. I heard loud voices. They were either closer than the first time or speaking more loudly than when I first noticed them.

As I reached the exterior of the house I realized Ping and Lala were blocking Duncan's way. I walked toward them in time to see two security men approach us to find out what was going on.

While John, the older man, stood back, Matias, the darker skinned of the two men, placed his hand on Ping's shoulder to restrain him and glowered at Lala. The foreigners were no match for the security men and they knew it. Duncan walked around them toward me thanking the guards. I was glad I had added his name to the security list.

"Thank you Matias, John." I knew their names from greeting them when I passed by the guardhouse and entrance on my walks. Our conversations were short and impersonal but at least I could communicate with them in English. They had always been polite, even friendly in the past. That day, I was so grateful I could have kissed them. I waved, realizing my enthusiasm and energy were showing and not caring one bit now that Duncan was with me.

As Ping and Lala walked away under the guards watchful gaze Duncan and I made our way to the house. Before we reached the steps I signaled to Duncan to follow me. It occurred to me that someone might be listening to the conversations in the house. It didn't make much sense since I was alone most of the time. Just in case it was a good precaution.

I stepped away from the trail stopping among the orange trees. With the adrenaline moment behind us we were both at a loss for words. I felt a little shy and self conscious, remembering that I must look a sight. With no laundry services I'd been washing my own clothes. When they were drying I wore the simple eastern style clothing Lala had given me. My hair must have looked a mess too. There was no mirror in the house and the small cheap comb Lala gave me had broken weeks earlier. So little had happened since then and at the same so much had changed for me. I felt like a different person. Well not so much a different person as an older and tired version of me.

Then we both started talking at the same time. Duncan stopped first and waited for me to speak.

So many emotions were battling to come out. I just managed to say two words, "You came." I sounded broken to my own ears. "I was afraid I might not ever see you again."

"I followed the car from the parking lot after the explosion and tried to get in here. Without my name at the gate, they just turned me away and denied you were even here. The next day, I got a call to pick up a letter at the guardhouse. It was from you saying that you and your mother were both safe and sound at a different location and that you were happy. It said you'd let me know when it was safe to have a visitor again and that I should stay away until that time."

I told him firmly "I didn't send you that note. As a matter of fact I got something similar from my mother telling me you were both unhurt and to stay put here. I can only guess that we have both been fooled by some kind of trick."

The terrible loneliness and sadness that had been my companion all those weeks threatened to take over. There would be time to catch up in the future; at least I hoped there would be. At that moment I had to figure out how to cure Mom. "There are so many things I want to talk about with you, but there's something urgent I have to do and I need your help."

"I'll help anyway I can. Name it."

Chapter 10

As I brought Duncan up to speed with my life since we last saw each other I saw his anger rise. It formed a shadow of sorts on his face. Although he sat still and quiet while I spoke I could sense the agitation fill his body. When I told him about Mom he was shocked.

"Zhao Tse told me she had minor injuries and was taken to a nearby hospital." As he said the words he began to realize the people we trusted had lied to us.

"That's the same thing he told me. I believed him, at first but it was so out of character for Mom to just leave without saying goodbye in person." I described more of what I saw and that she was in a coma at Methodist Memorial Hospital (I had seen the name printed on her patient record).

"Fastman, can you take me there? I want to see her in person, make sure she's okay." Using a nickname I'd given him when we met all those weeks earlier felt better than calling him plain old Duncan. It reminded me of the connection we had and of the good, if short, time we had spent together.

"Faster than a speeding bullet—" He made a face and flexed his arm muscles like a superhero, making me laugh. In spite of the anxiety I felt for Mom it was good to be with Duncan.

"I'm so glad you're here."

I must have looked tragic because he play punched me in the arm. "Who are you and where's the real Amy? The Amy I know doesn't say things like that. Maybe they replaced the real Amy with an alien pod."

I laughed again. "You're so right. No more goofing around Fastman. It's time to show off your fast walking ability or are you cracking jokes to distract me so I won't realize you've grown old since I last saw you and you can't walk fast anymore?"

The next thing I knew he'd walked behind me, hugging me with his arms around my midsection and we were speed walking through Coconut Grove. The residential area of The Grove, as locals called it, was not an ideal place to walk because it had narrow streets and few sidewalks. A few minutes into our walk Duncan stopped on a side street.

"How are you feeling?"

"I've felt better that's for sure. If what you want to know is whether the speed walking is making me ill, the answer is no."

"If you're sure—" I nodded yes impatient to see Mom and excited to be out of Douglas Estate. It was the first time in weeks that I was that far from the property not counting my dreamshifting dreams. I'd taken a few strolls into neighborhood streets and adjacent properties but I never strayed far for fear they would discover I was gone. It felt so good I was near crying. I didn't want Duncan to worry so I changed the subject.

"Do you know where Methodist Memorial is?"

"Not a clue." He pulled his smart phone out of his pocket and within minutes we were on our way again. The hospital website listed a main site and several satellite locations. The nearest to us was the main campus so we headed that way.

The hospital's main building was in a pretty wooded setting. As we approached it I was struck by the thought that if we hadn't known what it was we might have mistaken it for luxury lodging of some kind. The nearer we were the more signs of medical facilities there were. One sign pointed to the emergency entrance, others signaled the location of staff and visitor parking, rehabilitation, MRI, oncology and other departments and buildings.

In the main lobby, we found a map of the entire campus from which we made our best guess as to where Mom might be. After floundering around for what seemed like a long time but was only a few minutes we found her, several floors up tucked away in a secluded corner of the main building. She was just as she'd appeared in my dream. Her face looked peaceful but her condition was haggard. She was losing weight and her chart said she had to be moved often to avoid bedsores.

I kissed her forehead and whispered that I'd be back with a solution. This time I couldn't hold back the tears. Instead I made myself busy. I read the chart while Duncan kept watch in case any of the nurses appeared. Aside from the hard to read scribbles I'd seen on my previous visit there were only a few new notations, standard instructions and the anti-bedsore instructions I'd already seen. There was not much more we could do there. Seeing Mom like that made me wretched.

I figured after the long walk south from Coconut Grove to Pinecrest, where the hospital was located, Duncan must be hungry. "It seems you can still keep a modestly fast pace even with *moi* on board. You've earned some hospital grub."

"If it's all the same to you I'd rather eat just about anywhere else. Hospitals give me the creeps." He made exaggerated faces and started shaking for effect. I couldn't help but laugh. Although Mom's condition weighed me down I reminded myself that she was still alive. I'd feared the worst and although this was close it was better than dead. If she was in a coma there was still a chance she'd come out of it. I'd focus on that chance. I was nothing if not determined.

One of the reasons I liked spending time with Duncan was that we both laughed a lot when we were in each other's company. Since the last time we had spent a couple of days together had included excursions to Little Havana and South Beach, enough food to feed a village, an encounter with a fortuneteller, and an attempt on my life that ended up with

Duncan being hurt there was no telling what this time would bring. Past experience had shown me that in the midst of challenging situations we found time to look at the best angles as well as for oodles of giggles and laughter. If I had to weather a difficult situation Duncan was a top notch partner and I was thankful he was by my side.

.

Chapter 11

From the hospital we made our way to Paula's Place, a modest barbeque restaurant that the older woman at the information desk in the lobby recommended. She offered several options but when she spoke of the barbeque place her face lit up. Plus it was nearest to the hospital.

The building itself was not much to write home about and there was no air conditioning. It must be miserably hot in the summer and even in February, air conditioning would have helped reduce the humidity. On the other hand, the parking lot was boiling over with cars of all makes and models. We looked at each other and agreed it was worth a try, joining the short line of people snaking around the front of the building waiting for a table. The line was well managed and we had arrived in time for what seemed the second lunch wave. It didn't take us long to enter the restaurant.

Seating was on shared benches that spanned the length of the wall and faced matching built-in wooden tables. It was a no-frills type of place. The hostess led us to an end section facing the screen window and beyond it the full parking lot. In lieu of gazing at the not so stellar view we studied the menu. The smell of barbeque was inebriating. Until that moment I hadn't been hungry. I'd suggested we find a place to eat thinking Duncan would need to replenish the energy he'd spent on the speed walk.

Southern style waitresses complete with a drawl handled the crowd with practiced yet friendly efficiency. With the speed and expertise of someone used to eating out often Duncan picked what he thought were the best options to sample. When our waitress arrived we were ready. I wasn't sure what I'd like so I stuck with Duncan's suggestion, a full platter of baby back ribs and a corn on the cob. He had an iced tea and I had lemonade.

It was so noisy we weren't worried about someone hearing our strange conversation. Still we kept our voices low. After all superhuman walking and dreamshifting abilities were too fantastical for the average person to contemplate. I brought Duncan up to date on more of my life and the things that had happened since we had last seen each other and he did the same.

I was eyeing our departing neighbor's part empty plates with interest when Charlene, our server, arrived with mounds of food. It had been so long since I'd eaten a proper meal my mouth was watering. Duncan tucked in with gusto and I lost myself in lunch. The corn, set in a puddle of butter, was just right. I sprinkled a little salt and was good to go. The ribs were the kings of the party. They were fall-off-the-bone tender and oh so tasty. There was no need for the extra sauce Charlene had brought. The ribs and corn kept me so busy I barely made a dent in the French fries. The salad went untouched. Duncan had ordered two platters and a couple of side dishes including beans that looked good. There were few choices for dessert and by the end of the meal we didn't need any. By then the volume of the noise had gone down, less rock concert and more reggae as Mom's friend Genevieve used to say. It was time for a serious conversation.

Duncan listened to me with increased alarm. To his credit he waited until I outlined my plan and explained my reasoning without a single interruption.

"This is the same man we suspected might have sent someone to kill you nine weeks ago, right?" There was no point in arguing. I nodded. "The same man we think killed that woman who planned to accuse you of false crimes to send you to jail and out of her rental cottage? The father who was never there when you were growing up; but came looking for you when he wanted something?"

"Mmhmm."

"I'm not liking this plan."

"I had no idea. You hide it so well." I smiled. Not for the first time I was glad Duncan was with me. I'd have to negotiate and bargain to convince him. It meant he cared and for that I was more thankful than I realized. I could carry out my plan alone but it would be more dangerous. I'd been alone and felt abandoned all those weeks even though when I discussed it with Duncan I confirmed it wasn't true. I yearned for someone to have my back. I knew the protection was more emotional than anything. After all Duncan and I combined couldn't even tickle the power of our would-be opponent if my planned failed.

"I wish I could ask Mom for her opinion— Naw, she wouldn't agree to put me at risk even if she thought the plan had a chance of working."

"I need to think about this. You're worrying me. You're capable of doing this alone if I say no. I doubt I can convince you not to go forward unless I come up with a better plan. How about we do something else for a while to clear our minds?"

"What do you have in mind faster than fast man?" It was his turn to smile. He shrugged.

"Dunno— wanna go see some tourist sites? I'd suggest a swim at the beach but that didn't work out so well the last time." His expression turned serious.

A light bulb went on in my head like in the proverbial comic strips. "Yes, I've got a great idea. Let's go to the Beach."

"Really? You want to go swimming?" He was incredulous.

"Not exactly— but I do want to go to Miami Beach. Humor me." I batted my eyelashes with exaggerated motions until he burst into soft laughter. We had already settled our bill. Miami has one of the prettiest skies I've ever seen. That day it was a perfect medium blue with puffy white clouds flying high above. We walked toward the nearby office towers until we found a secluded spot. It seemed second nature for Duncan to find places to begin and end his speedy walks without being seen.

"Your chariot awaits, milady."

"Not a moment too soon either."

"If your ladyship would deign to inform me where we're going?"

"At the appropriate time young man you will be informed. This is a need to know mission and you don't need to know, yet." I winked and he smiled.

Without another word we stepped into speed walking position. It took some getting used to, seeing the city whiz by or perhaps it was the other way around, we were whizzing by the city. A short while later we arrived in South Beach, the southernmost section of the island of Miami Beach. Since he didn't know where we were headed Duncan stopped near a convenience store. It was a little worn and dated. The neighborhood around it had been modernized and rebuilt. He looked at me for directions.

"Do you remember the place where we bought cheap swim suits the last time?"

"Yes—"

"That's where I want to go, well, near that place anyway. That woman, the psychic, what she said sounded odd when we were at her shop but she was right. You saved my life. She called me Unelmoija, remember?" He nodded, uncertainty about the wisdom of the visit written all over his face. "I want to know what that means. Maybe she can tell me something about Mom or give me information to figure out if the plan I came up with to get her out of the coma will work."

"I'm not sure it's a good idea to retrace our steps that way, Amy. We don't know how the shooter found us when we were here before. One of the last places where we stopped before going swimming was that shop."

"You don't think it was the old woman?"

"No, but I don't know who shot at us either. It's better to be careful." His reasoning was sound.

I had been sitting in one place for too long and could not be careful any longer, not with my mother's life at stake. "Do you have a better idea? Can you think of a better plan? Do you know how we can get me out of that place and Mom out of the coma and the hospital?" I was half squeaking and half talking too fast and I knew it. It was not fair to snap at Duncan. He was my only friend. I didn't know what else to do.

"I don't have another plan. I'm sorry." I'd made him feel bad and all he was trying to do was make things better for me.

"Desperate times call for desperate measures and this is one of those times. Mom is getting worse. I have to do something even if it's risky for me. You can leave me somewhere safe, check out the place by yourself and make sure the psychic is there and that everything looks okay. You have a good sense for danger. I know you do." I might have been exaggerating a little. "If anything looks not to your liking we'll leave. If you find nothing to object to we'll go see her." He still was not buying it. "Tell you what; if she says my plan is no good I'll give it up. How's that for a tempting offer Speedy?"

"I can see your mind is set." I'd won the first battle. I kept quiet as the situation was still uncertain. Laughing might not win me brownie points when Duncan was so anxious. "I'm going to hold you to that. If she says you should drop your plan you'll drop it?"

"Yes, cross my heart and all that."

Duncan found a grocery store on Lincoln Road he liked for me to hang out until he reconnoitered the psychic's shop. It was near the sundry shop where we had gotten swim suits weeks earlier. A few minutes later, which felt like an eternity of waiting to me, he returned. We bought a couple of bottles of iced tea and water and went back into the sunshine to find my destiny or at least discover a little of it.

The shop was small, full of souvenirs, knick knacks and kitschy gifts. As we approached it a busload of tourists disembarked their transport and headed straight for the store. We walked up and down around the pedestrian street until the group left. Before my fearful companion could back out I tangled my arm around his and strutted toward the store.

Inside the shop was dark. It was not so much that it was without light as that by comparison to the bright sunlight of the outside it appeared dark. Once my eyes adjusted to the dimmer setting, I remembered my previous visit. I'd been browsing around with no aim or purpose. As I turned I noticed an older woman about to fall when a customer brushed by her in a hurry. I did what anyone would've done, reaching out to steady her.

"I thought you would be back," a voice I didn't recognize said. I turned but saw no one. Thinking a salesperson might have been speaking to a customer from the bus I said nothing.

"My words came to pass," the voice continued. It was not a question. She knew. This time the sound was nearer to me. I stood still, waiting. My patience was rewarded with the appearance of the older woman I'd seen before. She was wrinkled and yet she looked healthy. She smelled of tobacco and coffee even though I was too far from her to smell it. I knew.

She was short and full of repressed energy, like a cat ready to spring on its prey. She wore a long purple silk skirt and lighter colored blouse that matched the thread if not the color of the skirt. A necklace of large beads that looked like amethyst hung around her heavy set chest ending in a triangular shaped pendant. Her shoulder length gray hair was tied back with a barrette. Loose strands of hair circled her head like a halo although there was nothing angelic about her. The wear and tear of years and lessons learned hung on her like a badge of honor.

"Do not be afraid child. I mean you no harm and pose no threat to you or your handsome young man." I was not afraid. I was excited and nervous. I had so many questions. I didn't know what to ask first. "Very well, I shall speak until you find your tongue. Your life was in danger the last time you were here. It is obvious you escaped and for that I congratulate you. It was, it is, a formidable foe you face." I noticed she used the present tense, implying the foe was out there.

A squeak escaped my throat and she glanced at me.

"Have courage child. You have what it takes to succeed."

"Yes," I managed though my voice sounded strained.

"This time you fear for someone you love. Her life is in danger. She is ill. You are willing to risk your life to save her. Know this: Much more is at stake than your life in this matter. Her life, your life and the lives and well being of countless others will be affected by the decisions you make, by the path you choose."

I didn't understand and wanted to ask her to explain. Instead I managed to say, "You called me Unelmoija the last time I was here. What does it mean?"

"Ah, it is for you to decide. It is your destiny child. Have you not spoken with your mother? She cares for you and is the keeper of much knowledge." I shook my head bewildered. My mother had told me a little about the Weeia and my abilities. We hadn't had time for anything else. I didn't think there was any special destiny for me. I was just another teenage Weeia coming of age and finding her way. Okay, and my father was the enforcer for The Elders.

"That was the first time I heard the word spoken. I found out it means day dreamer in another language."

"Indeed it does. It means much more in your case. Like

the Death card in the Tarot deck which represents change or transformation, your moniker, your true name, means more than day dreamer. You should realize this, or you will eventually. What you may not know is that you have the heart of a brave warrior, the infinite kindness and wisdom of your mother, the maturity of an adult and the heavy weight of responsibility no one, let alone one as young as you, should ever have to bear. You also have the potential for untold power unlike anyone has ever seen. A dark force tempts you." My eyes grew wide and I shook my head from side to side. I whispered, "no." I didn't know of any dark force that tempted me. I'd spent weeks wearing the same outfit, washing my own clothes, eating like a Buddhist monk, not being tempted.

"If it has not tempted you yet, it will soon. You must temper your power or risk all. This dark force is complex. It is external and it is internal. The external force matters little unless you yield to your internal weakness. You can be a healer and unifier of your people or you may be their destroyer. You can be the beginning and the end. It is your decision."

I staggered back a step from the force of the knowledge I'd acquired. Her words frightened me. They sounded so certain, so final. Was it possible? Why had my mother never spoken of these things?

"I—" I remembered why I was there. I had to set my fears aside. I was there to get answers and answers she was giving me, though not the ones I sought. The one thing that mattered above all others was to save Mom.

"My mother is ill." I managed with a shaky voice.

"I know. She will die without intervention." Again with the certainty.

"I have a plan. Can you tell me if it will work?"

"Nothing is certain Unelmoija. Not even you, especially not your path." I was getting confused. A moment earlier, she had sounded certain my mother would die if I did nothing.

"I must save her. I'll do anything to save her."

"Anything? Be careful what you say child. Your words, your thoughts have more power than you realize."

I was feeling frustrated and desperate. I wanted her to tell me if I should go ahead with my plan, that it was the right path. More than anything I wanted reassurance. I was afraid. I had only Duncan to turn to for guidance, and he was opposed to my plan because it was too risky and there was no guarantee it would do anything for Mom.

"I can't give you the answer you seek. Only you can decide which fork in the road to follow child. I can tell you that your father did not order your death." A sigh escaped me. "That does not mean he is your friend or even that he loves you. I do not know the answer to those questions. He is broken and cannot be fixed no matter how much you try. Although he is filled with darkness and capable of hurting you, even killing you, he does not at this time wish your death."

Her words hit me like a physical blow. I didn't realize how much I longed for a father, someone who loved and cared about me. I guess I knew deep down some of what she said already. Hearing her say it made it real, inescapable. With her last words she retreated to a back room. I tried to follow but the door closed behind her and no amount of pushing had any effect. I thanked the door.

As we left I felt crestfallen. I'd sought easy answers and she'd given me none. Duncan sensed my mood and remained silent until I spoke.

"It's been a few hours since our last meal. I'm guessing those barbeque dishes are long gone." I tried for a smile though it may have come out more like a grimace. "How about we find a place around here for a snack?"

"Now that you mention it I'm feeling faint from lack of

nourishment." He made a goofy face. I guessed he meant to cheer me up.

"Shall we?" I pointed toward the other side of Lincoln Road. We had yet to explore the west side of the popular street and I figured there had to be at least one trendy place open.

"I thought you'd never ask." He handed me his arm and we walked in companionable silence for a few minutes until we came upon a vegetarian place that looked like a mix of unusual and nutritious. The menu outside listed quinoa platters, guacamole dips, fresh made fruit and vegetable juices, faux burgers, meatless lasagna and a bunch of other items I'd never heard of in my short life. I turned to see Duncan's reaction. I may be understating the expression on his face when I say he didn't look tempted.

Chapter 12

We kept walking until we reached Enzo's Eatery, an Italian cafe cum restaurant in a well trafficked corner. There was only one couple sitting in the outdoor terrace facing Lincoln Road which was not surprising given the hour. Even the early birds for dinner hadn't arrived. That seemed more Duncan's speed (no pun intended) than the vegetarian place. Within minutes we had our own table and were perusing the menu. After the barbeque feast I had for lunch I didn't think I'd be able to eat anything. To be polite I ordered a cold antipasto appetizer. Anything I didn't eat, I was confident Duncan would devour if invited.

"Are you okay?" He asked after a while. I'd been distracted thinking about the things the psychic had said and forgot to make conversation.

"Yeah, I guess. Did you hear what she said?" He'd been standing on the other side of the store when the woman approached me and I'd been so intent on what she was saying I wasn't sure how much of our conversation Duncan had heard.

"Some of it. I missed the beginning. Her tone of voice was so quiet it was hard to hear."

"That's odd. She sounded loud to me. I was glad we were the only two customers because her voice seemed so high I thought people outside the shop might hear her. Did you catch the last part, about my father?"

"Yes, I'm sorry. That must have been difficult to hear about your own father." He waited for me to speak. I didn't want to wallow in the pain of a bad father. I'd done that on and off for nine weeks. Now was the time to act not feel sorry for myself.

"She said my father didn't wish me dead. I'm sure he can

help bring Mom back. I can't explain how I know it but I do. I don't think he'll harm me."

"I also heard what she said about the risk you want to take to save your mother. She said 'there's much more at stake than you realize.'"

"What else can I do Duncan?" My eyes were stinging with unshed tears. "What would you do to save your mother?"

"I— I don't know." He lowered his head then turned away. "My mother and I aren't as close as you are with your mother. Still, I'd do everything in my power to save her."

"Even risk your life?"

"Yes." His voice was low. He sounded defeated.

"If you think I shouldn't do it, if you have another way, any ideas I'm willing to try those. If not—"

Duncan shook his head almost imperceptibly.

"Then I want to do this now while I still have the courage and you're with me. Agreed?"

"Yes, I'll be by your side."

"It's better if he doesn't know we're friends. I have the feeling he's possessive and jealous of his affections. Besides, surprise is our only weapon. His power is strong." I didn't want Duncan to know how afraid I was of my own father. I'd glimpsed a tiny sliver of his power the day we'd met. Behind the restraint and polite demeanor was a monster power barely kept in check by whatever rules he followed or laws he believed were worthy of respect. "He said all I have to do is think of him and he'll be by my side. I wonder how he can do that."

"I don't think he'll come in person. He'll respond to your mental call in your mind or as a projection if he has that ability."

"The way he said it made it seem like he would be with me."

He thought for a moment. "The ability to project allows

the person who has it to appear before someone at a distant location as a projection, a realistic one."

"It doesn't matter to me if he arrives riding a purple dragon, on the wings of giant doves or as a projection as long as he comes when I call." Duncan had a laugh. "I'll sit on one of the benches in the shade over there and think of him." I pointed at one of several empty benches within view of the cafe's terrace. "You can watch us from here without him being any the wiser."

To his credit Duncan agreed. With that I walked out of the restaurant and sat on a bench. I waved. I closed my eyes and quieted my mind as I did when I meditated. I thought of Thomas McKnight, my father. I remembered our first meeting as if it had been the day before instead of weeks earlier. His suntanned appearance made his blue eyes extra bright. They contrasted with his black hair with a hint of gray. I remembered that he wore an expensive suit and exuded the energy of a younger man.

The handsome man who had tracked me down when not even my mother knew where I was, wore authority like a second skin. I could tell he was used to being obeyed without question. He flinched ever so little at my irreverent attitude. The well dressed man with manicured hands who sat down to have espresso coffee with me at a neighborhood mart was a dangerous killer. All my instincts told me to be wary of him. The rational part of my brain told me he was not there to kill me. If he had been he wouldn't have needed to introduce himself. Besides, I could think of no reason why my own father whom I had never met would want to kill me.

At the same time, he had all the advantages. He knew who I was, where I was, what I was and so many things about me and my new dreamshifting abilities that I yearned to learn and understand. To say that I was stunned doesn't describe the surprise I felt on meeting my father. After the initial surprise, I don't know what I felt more anger, fear or sadness.

It was a bit disconcerting how his image was so fresh in my mind. In that moment, I felt him. It was an odd sensation as if he was in my head. I pulled back. My heart was racing. I felt spooked but I held steady, staying on the bench in case he decided to make an appearance. If Duncan noticed my nervousness he might come to check on me. That could be dangerous for him.

I didn't know how long it would take my father to contact me or arrive. I'd understood he'd hear my call right away but I didn't know where he was or how much time it would take him to reach me. Ten minutes passed. I was starting to think I'd made a mistake expecting that he'd respond or in contacting him at all. Perhaps the psychic was wrong and at that moment a killer for hire was setting his sights on me. I looked at my watch for the umpteenth time. Before I looked up I knew he was there.

"Amy, I was beginning to think you would never contact me." If what I saw was a projection it was a good one. He appeared pleased to see me. It was good to hear his voice for some inexplicable reason. I didn't want to like him.

"Thanks for coming. I thought I might have misunderstood what you said the day we met, about our bond."

"May I?" He pointed at the empty side of the bench.

"Yes, please." His power was such that I moved away as he sat not meaning to. I hoped he hadn't noticed. I had the feeling little escaped his watchful gaze.

"I am so glad to see you, so glad you reached out to me." I'd forgotten he enunciated with care and spoke without contractions. It sounded like older more polite English than the one we spoke today. "After we met I thought we would see each other again. I waited for your call. It never came. I have not felt your presence since that day. It was as if you had disappeared from the world." He paused as if waiting for an explanation. I wanted to believe he had nothing to do with the assassin that tried to kill me.

"Someone tried to kill me that day." He said nothing but his face showed surprise. "Nobody knew where I was, not even Mom yet someone found me and I took a shot at me. Your phone had GPS tracking capabilities."

"I—"

"Don't say you're not capable of killing someone. I know you're capable of that and much more." I interrupted him. I knew killing came with ease for him. What I wanted was for him to deny the accusation.

"I was going to say that I had no knowledge of that until you told me. I had nothing to do with the attempt on your life. What you say is true. I am capable and have done terrible things, things that your young mind would find intolerable and hard to understand. I will not deny that. I will not lie to you about that." He was pensive for a moment. "I do not make use of modern devices or electronics often in my everyday life. I have little need. I asked a trusted colleague and disciple to assist me. It seems he was not as trusted as I thought. I assure you—" his tone became tighter in that part of the sentence "—that I will look into this and the culprit or culprits will be dealt with most— well just know I will take care of it."

An awkward silence engulfed us. He was observing me and I was fidgeting in my seat, trying to find a way past my anger and hurt feelings to ask for his help.

"You look ill Amy. You are too thin, your clothes are worn. What has happened to you? Has someone hurt you?" Was that concern in his voice? I dared not think it was or I would lose my way. I had to stay strong.

"That doesn't matter." I managed to say with not a small amount of effort. As I remembered the past few weeks of loneliness, hunger and fear my emotions threatened to get the better of me.

"It does. Tell me who hurt you, what happened. That must be why you contacted me." He ended in a half statement and half question.

"Yes, the last nine weeks have been difficult for me." I stopped to regain my composure before my voice broke. I took a moment before going on. "I won't deny that. That's not why I called you. It's not for me that I need help." I went on before I lost my nerve. "Mom is in a coma. I think she's been that way for nine weeks. I don't know the details." I was aware that I was speaking at a break neck speed but I couldn't help it. "I called to ask if there's anything you can do. I'm afraid she's going to die." I stopped there as I heard my voice quiver with emotion.

My father's arm moved toward me as if to console me and I flinched, moving back in fear. He said nothing, just dropped his arm.

"I know you wanted something from me when you introduced yourself. Tell me what it is and if I can I'll give you what you want in exchange for you saving Mom's life." I heard myself speak, unaware of giving the command. My voice was not its usual steady self but at least it had stopped quivering and I was not crying, anymore.

My father's face showed a mix of emotions. I didn't know him well enough to recognize everything he was feeling. I knew sufficient to see or sense deep roiling anger, pity, helplessness, and dark fear. The depth of the anger was a surprise. The pity and helplessness were unwanted, useless. The fear was unexpected. Time passed as we sat next to each other on the bench, my father silent while I wondered if I'd made a terrible mistake.

"Say something, please." I beseeched.

He turned to look at me with something between sadness and anger. "I do not know what, if anything, I can do to help your mother. I am not a doctor. I know nothing of these matters." He was speaking a half truth. "I will assist you without recompense. I will help you, if I am able, because you are my daughter." This seemed true. "I know you do not trust me. After what you have told me and what happened before we met I cannot blame you. I hope in time that changes. For now, I accept the limited relationship open to us." I nodded not trusting myself to say anything nice, wondering what he'd offer now.

"Amy, I must go. I left in the middle of a delicate situation to be by your side. I would offer to take you home or to safety but I imagine you called me to this place to avoid letting me know where you live." I said nothing and he continued. "Tomorrow morning at dawn, contact me from your mother's location and we will deal with this together. Can you do that?"

"Yes, thank you." My voice was still not normal and I felt myself shiver although it was warm. I watched my father as he got up from the bench, looked into my eyes and walked away. After two blocks he turned a corner and I could no longer see him.

Chapter 13

We waited a few minutes to make sure my father was gone before Duncan took me back to the estate. Since on a regular day I was on my own most of the time there was no reason for Ping and Lala to have noticed my absence except for their clear objection to Duncan's visit earlier that day. Although it seemed the threat to my life hadn't come from my father, I didn't dare leave the estate until we had sorted the situation with my mother. If I died now, there would be no one to look after her. To avoid conflicts Duncan left me in the main house, promising to return before sunrise. That would allow us enough time to make our way to the hospital and for me to contact my father at dawn as he had requested.

Everything went according to our plan. When I arrived at the main house I found my usual platter of rice and a bowl of bouillon along with a ripe banana. I learned during my stay at Douglas Estate that I have a deep dislike for ripe bananas. Weeks of meager meals with no meat should have meant I would eat the modest lunch they brought. After everything I'd eaten that day I had trouble facing another one of Ping's platters. Given the strong food smell he carried I was sure Ping was the cook. I tried not to think of how dirty his hands and nails were or of the filthy kitchen I had visited in my dreamshift when I faced my single daily ration of food. I let the platter sit untouched, thinking I might eat it in the morning before Duncan arrived.

Too many thoughts were circling in my mind. I replayed the events of the day, my conversations with Duncan, the things the psychic had told me, and everything I could remember about the encounter with my father. I went to bed feeling hopeful that with Duncan and my father's help, Mom would come out of the coma. Maybe in time, and with her by my side, we could figure out a way to get me out of Douglas Estate and its uncomfortable living conditions.

Either I was getting better at controlling my dreamshifting or luck was with me because it was a restful and dream free night. I'd always been a morning person. I liked the hours before sunrise when the air was still and quiet. I woke up on my own and readied myself for Duncan's arrival. We had decided he'd bypass the guarded entrance and reach the house through the trail we had taken the day before. It was not that we had anything to hide but it would appear odd that he was visiting me before dawn.

We made good time to the hospital. There were fewer cars on the road at that hour than later in the day, making it easier to cross streets and intersections than during the heavy traffic hours. The sky was clear and the temperature cool. Miami had chilly days in February. This was one of them. I was thankful that Duncan brought a sweater for me.

"Handsome and thoughtful."

"Don't get used to it young lady."

I was pretty sure visiting hours didn't include predawn. We snuck into my mother's room rather than explain to the staff who we were and what we were doing there. Telling them that we planned on bringing my mother out of the coma would sound unconvincing. Still, I was certain it could be done and felt better now that my father had agreed to meet me. True, he'd made no promises but he hadn't denied it was possible either.

What to do about Duncan? There was nowhere for him to hide in the room. We thought of the bathroom but my father was sure to notice his presence. The room two doors down from my mother's was empty. It had been occupied when Duncan and I visited the hospital. Whoever had been there had been transferred and a new patient hadn't arrived. The best part was that the staff had no reason to enter the room.

"Are you sure about this?" Duncan asked me, concern in

his voice. "I can take care of myself. You don't need to protect me from your father." My father was one of the most powerful men of our race and one of The Elders, the ruling class who made up and enforced most of the norms of our society. Duncan, kinder and a better person overall than my father, was no match for him even if he could easily outrun him. Unfortunately, even Duncan can't outrun a dreamshifter. We both knew that. I didn't want to hurt his feelings by pointing it out.

I didn't think my father would be happy to know that Duncan and I'd become friends. I wasn't sure what he'd do or how he'd react. The best thing, I thought, was to keep Duncan out of my father's way, at least until the situation with my mother was resolved. After that, there would be no need for me to be around my father or for Duncan to be in the middle like he was at that moment.

"If I need anything I'll call for you. I'm sure it'll be fine. You saw that yesterday he didn't say or do anything threatening. He could've taken me or killed me if that was what he wanted. I'll feel better knowing you're out of his reach."

"Have it your way." He didn't look convinced.

Once Duncan checked that the nurses rotation had ended he got settled in the empty patient room. I sat down in one of the two chairs in Mom's room. Closing my eyes like the day before, I quieted my mind like I did when I meditated. Then, I thought of my father. This time he just appeared. I was expecting it. The strange thing was that he looked real. My brain said he was a mirage. My eyes told me that if I reached out and touched him he'd be flesh and blood.

"How do you do that? Are you really here?" I couldn't help asking.

He smiled. "That is my secret." I noticed that when he smiled his face softened from the harsh threatening appearance he wore most of the time. "I will see you in thirty minutes Amy. Can you wait that long?" I nodded yes and he disappeared as if he'd never been there in the first place.

I checked the hall before heading out to tell Duncan what had happened. There was a lot of activity near the floor's central desk. I assumed it was a shift change. Fearing I might be seen I opted to stay put. I'd have to do a lot of explaining if someone caught me in Mom's room. I found it odd that she was listed as a Jane Doe in her medical chart. Master Tse had said she'd been taken to the hospital and was alright. I assumed he or his staff had checked in on her at the hospital. He'd lied about her condition. It shouldn't have surprised me that he'd done nothing to assist her which is what it looked like. Assuming he'd checked on her was my fault. I wanted to believe the best of people.

It would be better if I filled Duncan in later. Instead, I went to Mom's side. She looked different, not like herself. The expression or the lack of expression on her face gave her an odd appearance. Even through the sheets I could tell she'd lost weight and her skin had an unhealthy tone. Her hair fell limp from her head and her unpolished nails looked like they had been gnawed off by a hungry beaver instead of trimmed with care.

My eyes filled with tears. I was terrified Mom wouldn't snap out of her coma, that she would leave me alone. I reminded myself that for both of our sakes I had to be strong. Other than dear Duncan there was no one else trustworthy to be there with me. I had to do what needed doing. There was no choice. I refused to cry or wallow in the fears that threatened to overcome me. I had to be calm and have my wits about me when my father came back. It wouldn't do for me to be a basket case when the Dark Lord that he was returned. I sat back in the seat to meditate while I waited for my father to reappear.

By the time he arrived, twenty nine minutes later, I'd

calmed down somewhat. This time, he came through the door. He looked almost the same as he had earlier except there was a kind of higher definition to him. I rose from my seat as he entered and took two steps in his direction whispering "you came" as if Mom would wake up from her coma because she heard my voice. If only that was all it took. Two long strides brought him to my side and to my surprise the hugged me. He smelled of metal, smoke and things that frightened me. At the same time, the scent was, in a vague way, familiar as if he had hugged me before, as if I knew that smell. I concluded that he smelled like my father. In that I found, for the briefest of moments, immense comfort.

I knew at least to a small degree what he was and it was less than good. I knew his motives were at best divided and at worst sinister. Still, for some reason seeing him made me feel better and safer than I had moments before his appearance. My father was with me and between us we would find a way to cure Mom. Whatever other issues he brought would wait until we solved Mom's problem. As long as my mother was well again I thought I could handle whatever came my way, even Master Tse and his minions. I allowed my hopes to rise. In the back of my mind I realized it could all be an illusion, not that he was there but that he was going to help us. For the moment, I held on to the more promising possibility, the one that got my mother out of the coma.

Chapter 14

My father spent some time studying Mom's medical chart, like someone used to such documents. His expression darkened. He turned to me. "It says nine weeks ago your mother was injured in an explosion. Were you with her when that happened? Were you also injured? How is it that you waited so long to call me?"

"I—" I didn't know what to say. I didn't know how much information I could share with him without placing us in danger. I'd have been concerned about putting the people who gave me shelter in harm's way except that they had turned out to be not so nice. I'd become convinced that they had been drugging me, perhaps even poisoning me. My face must have looked unhappy because he added. "I understand that you do not trust me. If you want me to help you, you must be honest with me." He faced me, looking calm and patient. I got the feeling he wouldn't budge an inch until I responded to his question. The most important thing at that instant was Mom's health. Whatever it took to make her better I was willing to do as long as it didn't result in innocent people being hurt.

I remembered my father's protectiveness toward me, how he'd murdered a woman who had threatened my safety with false accusations that could've led to my being charged with a crime. I managed to escape her before my father and I even met. That didn't keep him from making an example out of her to anyone in Weeia circles. Mess with my daughter and you mess with me.

My feelings were conflicted on that issue. I'd grown up believing I was human, respecting and fearing human laws and the human justice and police systems. On the other hand, I'd discovered first hand that those systems were imperfect and many innocent people were left unprotected and sometimes hurt because of the flaws in the system and the unscrupulous people who took advantage of it. My father had played judge, jury and executioner to protect his status among the Weeia. At the same time, he'd rid the world of a harmful woman who seemed well past redemption.

"We arrived together, but Mom dropped her purse and Duncan was helping her sort it out. I walked to the limo and everything exploded with noise and confusion. When I reached safety they kept me from going out to her. They gave me a letter from Mom saying it had been just bruises and bumps; that she'd been to the hospital and was released. I don't even know why I believed it. I didn't question what they said or the letter they gave me until recently. They sent one to Duncan as well. I only just found out she was in a coma. I contacted you as soon as I was able." I felt my anger burn and my eyes sting. I realized some of what I was saying might not make sense to my father.

"Wait here." He stalked out.

I paced the room, feeling like I'd done something wrong, like I'd failed Mom by not finding a way to run out, by not going to the hospital that day. Strong hands, of the muscled security guards, had kept me inside the car. It didn't help matters that I'd been stunned by the blast and my hearing numbed for several hours. I had been helpless, unable to go to her, I reminded myself. Then that stupid forged letter fooled me into staying put and accepting everything.

A few minutes later my father returned looking grim. "Nine weeks ago, your mother was brought to the emergency room after an explosion in Coconut Grove, alone. By the time an ambulance arrived she had lost a lot of blood. She was admitted and treated for her injuries before she fell into a coma. Your mother had several thousand dollars in cash but no identification or wallet on her. No one has been to see her and nobody has called to ask about her since then.

Whoever told you she was safe lied to you. You cannot trust them." He didn't say "You can trust me" but his meaning was clear. What he said confirmed much of what I knew already or had concluded on my own.

"Tell me something new," I snapped. "What I need from you is a way to get her out of the coma, a way to cure her."

He went on with the safe and trust thing. "You could have been injured. Do you see that? The people you are with are not your friends."

"I get that. Neither are you. If it wasn't because I was afraid that you had tried to have me killed, because you were one of the few people who could know where I was because of the cell phone GPS I —" I didn't want to make more accusations. That was not why I had called him.

We were quiet for a few minutes. I broke the silence. "I can't fix what happened nine weeks ago and I don't want to talk about those people, or you or who I do or don't trust. Can you cure Mom? Yes or no?" I emphasized the last question. It was the only thing that mattered to me at that moment. It was the only reason I'd dropped my guard and called him even though I was part repulsed and part afraid of him.

A sad look took over his face. "I am sorry. I do not know how or if she can be cured."

"Then why did you come here in the first place?" I spat the words, angry that he'd led me on and now was pulling the carpet of hope I sat on from under me. I didn't expect an answer.

"I thought I might be able to help. I thought there might be a mistake and she might not be so out of reach."

Undaunted I went on. I'd allowed myself to believe in a cure and this hopelessness so soon was not what I expected. I wanted to hurt him the way I was hurting. "I thought you were this powerful, mighty Elder that could do anything. I thought you had almost unlimited powers and that's why people fear and hate you so much. What can you do? If you can't help my mother you're no good to me. I'm sorry I ever called you."

I must have been screaming louder than I realized because a nurse knocked on the door and came in. She was an older woman with frizzy curly hair that circled her face like a lion mane. Her air of authority dimmed as she saw my father.

"Mr. McKnight. I'm sorry to bother you. I heard the screams as I was walking down the hallway to check on Mrs. Torres. Is everything okay?" She gave me a stern look.

"Yes, Nurse Baxter. I am grateful for your interest. This is a difficult situation for my daughter Amy as you can imagine." His voice was soothing and authoritative. "Do not worry. Rest assured I will deal with this. You may continue with your duties and forget what you heard. I am sure you have other patients and work to attend to right now."

"Very well, if you say so. I do have a lot of work today." She walked out without hesitating.

As she left my father turned to me. "Amy, keep your voice low to avoid attracting the staff's attention. We have enough to worry about without becoming unwelcome visitors."

"You're not the boss of me. You're nothing to me. I'll say whatever I want whenever I want and you have nothing to say about it. You were never there when I was growing up so you have no right to say anything now." I lowered my voice. My anger was cooling but my pride made it difficult to admit I'd been at fault. I gave him credit that he said nothing in reply to my challenge.

A long silence followed. I returned to the seat I'd occupied before my father's arrival. There had to be something we, no I, could do. It was clear I was alone in this as my father didn't seem willing to explore options. "What about reaching her through a dream? I'd dreamshift until forever regardless of the consequences she warned me about if it would get her back. Is that possible?"

"I do not know." His voice was small, unlike the tough Elder he was to everyone else. "How would you find her? In her coma she is somewhere unknown to us. Even if you found her, which would be near impossible, you might get stuck with her wherever she is and unable to return. Her condition is getting worse. It would be dangerous." I realized he was concerned about me.

"If there's a chance it will work, I have to try. I'll begin right now. Is there anything I should know before I begin?" Although I had a rudimentary knowledge of my abilities and how to use them, I felt calmer now that I'd chosen a path forward. Even if it was risky, if it meant I might be able to help Mom, I would do it. I was not bluffing. My father seemed to sense that I spoke the truth.

"You are as brave as your mother and as impetuous and foolish as I was at your age." His voice softened a smidgen. "I believe you would try to do it alone." He was quiet for a moment. "There is no need for you to make this journey on your own. I will assist you. My knowledge of dreamshifting is vast. With any luck your abilities will be quite similar to mine and I can guide you."

I was taken aback by what seemed out of character for him. "Why would you do that?"

"Although you may have a hard time believing it I want to be your father in more than name. I do not know if we can succeed, the odds are against us. If you wish it, if you plan to risk your life to do it I can do no less than to go with you."

"Doesn't that mean you'll be risking your life too?"

"It does. Are you sure you want to go forward with your plan to find your mother in a dream even though it could mean that we dream ourselves into a coma with her with no way home?"

"Yes." There was nothing to add. That was what I wanted

and the sooner the better. I sensed Mom slipping away. Like a tire leaking air soon there would be little left and it would become flat. I didn't know where the comparison came from. It must have been from the tire changing lessons Kat had given me. It seemed that had happened in another lifetime.

"Very well. I will assist you. However, this is not a safe place. We will need to move your mother to another location where we can dreamshift in safety without the threat of attacks." My mouth opened to object and no words came out. It hadn't occurred to me that we might be attacked. It made sense. After all, Mom was in the hospital because unknown people had tried to blow us up. Someone Duncan had thought trustworthy had betrayed me, drugged and maybe poisoned me for unknown reasons. Before that someone had tried to kill me. He was right to be concerned.

"Where?" I had so many questions I was having trouble getting them out in a coherent way. "How can we move her if she's in a coma? Is it safe? How will we convince the hospital to let us take her?"

"I will deal with the hospital. Do not worry. Hospitals, even good ones, are businesses like any others. They have to stay within budget; they have to keep to the bottom line. Having your mother here as a Jane Doe is costing them thousands of dollars a day in expenses that no one has covered. They would be happy for her to leave so they can replace her with a paying patient. All we have to do is make it easy for them to accept. I have resources at my disposal. I will find a safe place for us to transfer her and hire any medical staff required."

It occurred to me that Mom might not want to be moved to a location controlled by my father. I had little choice if we were to rescue her from the coma.

"You have to promise me that you will bring her back here if her life is in danger or if I ask you to for any reason." I gave him what I hoped was a threatening look. He agreed.

"I will need to leave to make the necessary arrangements. Do you wish to come with me?"

"If you don't need me I'd prefer to stay with Mom."

"Very well Amy. Call your young friend then to keep you company. I will feel more comfortable knowing you are not alone."

I was surprised. "Wha—"

"Did you think I would not make a thorough security check after the attacks on you and your mother? I saw Duncan Bittersdorp loitering around in the other room."

"I didn't know Weeia could sense other Weeia," I half asked half said for lack of something else.

"They cannot. But I never go into this type of situation without checking the nearby rooms. If you have the sort of abilities I expect, you will be able to learn this technique." This supernatural Weeia stuff was getting on my nerves. I walked over to the empty patient room, taking care that none of the staff saw me, and brought Duncan up to speed.

"You don't have to do this Fastman. It's not your responsibility to look after me let alone to face my Dark Lord father for inspection."

"I know that. I want to be there for you. Besides I feel terrible that the situation at Douglas Estate is not what I promised. I trusted people I shouldn't have and that created a bad situation for you." I hadn't told Duncan about the drugging or about my suspicions about poison yet. He'd seen my living conditions and met Ping and Lala. He had a partial idea of my life there. If I'd told him about the rest, he'd have insisted that I leave Douglas Estate that same day, but where would I go?

Until my skills were stronger or I had somewhere else to go I had to stay there. I didn't want him to get hurt again. The last time we had been together he'd taken a bullet to keep me safe and suffered through an explosion. Thanks to his abilities he had recovered. The next time he might not be so lucky. "Even if I didn't like you I'd help you to make up for that. It's easier to deal with your father because I like you. You're like the sister I never had." He gave me a lopsided grin that made me feel a thousand times better. If I'd been in his shoes I'm pretty sure I'd have been nervous to see my father.

Chapter 15

"Nice to see you Duncan," my father said with a bit of sarcastic sneer in his voice. Duncan puffed himself up and faced the older man as if he had no cares in the world.

"It's a pleasure to see you too McKnight. As much as I enjoy admiring your looks and witty repartee I'm here for your daughter whether you like it or not." I thought my father, who didn't seem to play well with others, would blow a gasket. Instead he seemed to think it over.

"How is it possible? You are opposites. Your energies should push you apart. Do you not feel uncomfortable in each other's company?"

Before Duncan had a chance to say anything I chimed in. "That's our secret." Two could play the same game. My father's "hmmf" was so soft I almost missed it. I smiled. Duncan, who had been in the other room during my earlier exchange with my father looked puzzled but said nothing trusting my judgment.

"Very well, young man. I hope you are as able protecting her as you are mouthing off. The time may come when you will be tested." Duncan, rather than play the tough guy to face off with the bigger tough guy that was my father, opted to show off in a care free wise cracking role. "Oh, no not the 'be tested' time." He replied with an exaggerated gesture that had me in stitches in spite of the somber mood I'd been in earlier. He looked at me to make sure everything was as it should be and I smiled. I chose not to tell my father that Duncan had already saved my life once, that he had been injured during the explosion or that I trusted young Mr. Bittersdorp far more than I trusted the man who had given me life.

Deciding to quit while he was ahead my father took his

leave promising to return the following day at the same time. If all went as he expected by then he'd have found a place with all the medical requirements where we could move my mother. It would also be safe for us while we dreamshifted in search of my mother's conscious mind. He refused to estimate how many trials we would have to make or how long the process would take. He reminded me that we didn't know what condition her mind would be in after nine weeks in a coma. I let him know I understood, thinking we would cross that bridge when we got there. I was relieved that he had agreed to go along with me on the impossible mission.

"Amy, are you sure you're comfortable with your father's plan? Aren't you afraid?" Duncan said concerned as soon as my overbearing father was gone.

"I'm sure I'm not comfortable Fastman. If I had any other idea that was better I'd do that." I stopped for emphasis and to let the funny phrasing sink in. "I don't trust my father but, and it's a big but, he's a powerful man. As an Elder he has huge resources and I have none. If anyone can help me help Mom it's him. I don't like that I had to ask him. I'm more than surprised that he said yes. What we're planning is risky for him too. I'm still not sure why he agreed. I accepted before he had a chance to change his mind."

He looked at me, understanding and maybe a dash of pity, showing on his face.

"I also don't like that we'll be in his space once we move my mother but I don't know how else we can do what we need to do. I want to believe I'm safe from the killer but we still don't know who's trying to kill me or why. When I'm dreamshifting, I'm defenseless and so is my father," I said.

"Don't worry too much. You'll drive yourself crazy. I'll stay with you through the whole thing. I know I can't defeat your father but maybe between us we can outsmart him if nothing else works." Hearing Duncan I let out a breath I'd been holding. It was an enormous relief to know he planned to stay by my side. I didn't dare ask him. I knew he had duties and didn't want to impose or endanger him, again. After all he didn't have any responsibility to me, we weren't related. We were united only by a new friendship.

"Are you sure? I don't want this to make problems for you. You have lots of things to take care of and I can do this alone."

"A wise woman, my mother, told me once: Friends are the people who care about you and are there for you when you need them, not when it's convenient. I'm your friend. You need me now. I'll make time and we'll do this together. I'll need to sort out some things before tomorrow to make sure nothing important falls through the cracks while I'm with you. Let's get something to eat before I take you back to the estate, and I'll pick you up tomorrow so we can meet your father."

Lunch was less fun than usual. We were both distracted and although Duncan never said anything I had a feeling he needed to be somewhere else.

"What only three sandwiches and two chocolate shakes? You're getting old on me Fastman. Next thing you know we'll be eating the same amounts or better yet I'll eat more than you."

"That'll be the day," he laughed almost spilling some of the shake on the table. He caught the glass in time and steadied it while taking a bite of the last sandwich. "I'm not sure you should go back to the estate after what I saw and how aggressive that father and daughter team were. Are you sure you'll be okay?"

"I've managed to survive nine weeks without, well with little harm," that was too close to the truth. "I should be alright a few more days." I left out my question, besides where would I go? I could ask Duncan to take me wherever he was staying but I didn't know where that was and there was a chance it would cause him trouble. I was not his responsibility. He was being such a good friend with everything he had done already.

Chapter 16

The rest of the day was uneventful. After Duncan dropped me off at Douglas Estate, I walked to the waterside Cabana to meditate for a short while before returning to the main house. I should have washed my clothes but was too tired. I was also concerned my clothes wouldn't dry in time and I'd have to wear the ugly ones Lala had given me to the hospital.

I was so absorbed with my own thoughts that I missed the signs that other people had been in the house. If I had paid attention to my surroundings I would've seen the woman's handbag on the table next to the foreign newspaper. I might have picked up on the expensive over spicy sweet woman's perfume, the man's cologne with a lime finish or the strong cigarette smell that lingered in the air. Instead, I was surprised to hear voices. As I turned the corner into the sitting room I saw a well dressed couple. He was standing on one side looking distracted and speaking on his cell phone. She was flipping through the pages of a fashion magazine, not paying attention.

"You must be Amy," she said when she saw me. An odd smile stretched across her face. It made me think of the cat that had swallowed the canary. "I'm Marga Assugranes and that's Marcus, my husband. We're the owners of Douglas Estate." She got up and glided over to where I was standing to air kiss my cheeks and grasp my hands as if I was an honored guest that had arrived at her house for tea and cookies instead of a virtual prisoner in a neglected home she spared no effort supervising.

"I'm so glad you're safe," she said though her tone was angry rather than concerned. There was a slight accent I couldn't place. It reminded me of foreigners who tried so hard to sound American that they came across as somewhat fake. They had an exaggerated way of pronouncing words that made them sound unnatural. "Mr. Tse couldn't find you when we arrived and we were beginning to worry. It's best to stay within the property for your own good. Where were you?"

I balked at her question and her demanding tone. Keeping a calm demeanor I reminded myself I was a guest at her home, catching the acerbic reply before it reached my lips. "I was at the Cabana until a little while ago when I returned to wash my clothes."

Mollified she wrinkled her nose and looked me up and down as if I was a cow she was going to sell at auction. My worn and less than stylish clothes didn't match the high fashion expensive attire she and her husband wore with ease. As if noticing that I could see her she adjusted her expression. "It would be lovely if you joined us for dinner. We won't stay in Miami long but I had to make time to meet you. It's such a pleasure."

She didn't wait for an answer, making me realize she expected me to do her bidding without question. It made me wonder if she was behind the tea, lights and drugging that had been affecting me. Did she think I would follow orders because I was drugged? I had assumed it was the staff's doing, never thinking the owners were behind my discomforts. If so, she would've anticipated that I would be compliant. I decided to follow along and find out what she wanted. I waited for her to take the lead.

Her faded beauty might have been striking if it hadn't been for the marks of bitterness that lined her features, darkening her exotic face. Although her cinnamon colored skin had an unhealthy sheen I imagined at one time it must've been one of her most attractive features.

"We'll see you at 7:30 p.m. on the terrace for drinks."

When I arrived they already had made good headway with their drinks. "Care for a scotch or do you prefer vodka?" She asked when she saw me, wrinkling her face in undisguised distaste once again. Both had changed for dinner, making me feel like an ugly duckling with my tattered clothes.

"Marga dear. She's a young girl. She probably prefers sweet cocktails or rum," her husband said as if to sooth her. While he wasn't handsome in a classic sense he was attractive with rugged features. He was stout and muscled underneath his wrinkle free linen suit. It struck me that in the short amount of time since their arrival they had worn more clothes than I owned and that he had his suit pressed already. There was no way a linen suit would look that way after escaping a suitcase.

"Of course. I'll have Mr. Tse prepare something for her." Her voice had taken on an over sweet tone as if pleasing me was her number one priority.

"Better not. That's way beyond his skill set. I'll prepare something for her." I was about to say I didn't want a cocktail and decided it was better to accept the drink. While she stared out into the night I watched him blend lemonade and a clear liquid with a syrupy consistency then add a tiny amount of dark rum and ice to the tall glass. He handed it to me when he was done. I nodded to show my appreciation. When I looked at his face I saw lines of age and something else perhaps sadness.

"I was in a mood for steak. You don't mind, do you darling?" Marga said to Marcus.

"Of course not. The steak in the States is excellent," he said just as his cell phone rang. He picked it up winning a furrowed brow from Marga. He was on the phone discussing what sounded like business a long while. She finished her drink and made herself another. She topped up her husband's drink and glanced at mine which was full. After tasting it I had left the rest untouched. I didn't want alcohol to muddle my mind while I was around them. All my instincts told me that in spite of the welcoming attitude they, Marga in particular, weren't my friends.

"It's time for dinner," she said when he hung up. She rose from her seat and we followed her.

I was surprised to see a dining table set up on the terrace with candles. As we approached I noticed a pretty dinner service adorned the table with real silver, crystal glasses and cloth napkins. There was bread in a basket, butter and a bottle of red wine in a cooler. It was a bit surreal to see such an elegant set up given the primitive conditions I had experience during my stay there.

When we sat down I noticed her eyes were bloodshot. I had already seen her down two drinks. Sometime when I wasn't looking a fresh one had appeared in her hand.

Ping and Lala, somewhat more presentable than usual, served a green salad first. I ate my salad while Marga and Marcus talked about work. Neither of them had eaten much when Ping returned to clear the plates.

"So dear," Marga turned to me. "have you had a nice stay here?"

I might've gagged on my reply if Marcus hadn't intervened to ask her about a decision that was pending for a conference they were attending.

"I understand perfectly why you're running away from your father, you know," Marga said looking at me as if she alone had the answer to a difficult puzzle. "My father is like yours, an egomaniac who has always wanted to rule my life." She sounded sincere. "That's why we were happy to offer you shelter even though there is some danger for us of course." She went on as if remembering. "It's taken me all my life to liberate myself from him. Ever since I can remember he has pushed his views on me. He's wily, you know. He never forced me to do anything. Instead he manipulated me into agreeing. First, decades earlier it was a loveless marriage of convenience for him. I put up with the domineering, selfish human husband he chose for me, and bore him two girls. I tolerated his unbearable personality for far too long. Because of my father's insistence on the wedding I gave up my dream to become a doctor. I still resent my father and my first husband for that decision. Many things have changed since then."

Marcus reached out to hold her hand while she continued. "When I could no longer stand to be around my husband Josef and his brats I walked out, leaving my father to pick up the pieces. If he wanted Josef's influence, his contacts and his business, let him deal with him himself. I was no longer his willing pawn. I wasn't able to live with those girls either. Every time I saw them they were a reminder of my lost illusions and the best years of my youth gone never to return. It was as if they were someone else's children, not mine." She sighed.

"After that I picked myself up and dusted myself off and recovered from that dull marriage. As soon as I could, I went back to college. I worked hard and paid attention. Thanks to all that I had learned about business at my father's lap, I did well in my undergraduate studies, graduating a year early. I decided to postpone my medical studies. They would take too long and cost too much money. Medical school was expensive. I needed to make my own fortune and become independent from my father."

Marcus signaled Ping and Lala to go away when arrived to check in on us. She went on. "He had to impose his will there too. When I was ready to attend graduate school he bribed me into starting a business instead of pursuing a master's degree in business administration at one of several top universities where I had been offered admission. I still remember his words: 'You want to get an MBA? Pay for it yourself. It's a waste of money. You learn everything you need on the job. You want your own business? I'll finance any business you want to start.' In the end, I took the easy road. He gave me five million dollars that same day with which I started the import/export business that we own today."

"She's always had a good head for business," Marcus said with evident pride.

"Marcus, a Material henki with excellent skills, was the best match for me. I was never meant to be with a human," she said, spitting out the words. "His forgery skills and my ability to imbue objects with emotional energy complement each other perfectly." Marcus looked uncomfortable with her words but didn't interrupt her. As if reading his body language she spoke. "It doesn't matter now darling. It won't matter if the girl knows." That sounded ominous to me. She turned to me and continued. "We found many ways to use our skills to advance our business interests and cut out competition. We share the same drive to succeed. Unlike the girls I left behind along with my failed first marriage, Marcus and I planned and awaited the birth of our boys with eagerness." There was genuine fondness in her eyes as she smiled.

"During the boom years of the economy, feeling overconfident we extended our investments beyond our core strengths. The world had been our oyster until the music stopped. We discovered big losses would force changes in our lives. Even though my father forgave me for leaving Josef and the girls he won't bail us out. Money is sacred for him, you know. He feels we wasted ours." She stopped for a moment, a faraway look in her eyes.

"None of that matters now that our boys are gone," Marga's anger was all over her face. "I wish I had spent more time with them when I had the chance. I was too busy working to take time off to be with them."

"We were always traveling and developing our business when the boys were growing up," Marcus said. The softness in his tone was tender, loving. It was meant for her. I felt in the middle and wondered, not for the first time, why she was telling me about her life.

"Juan was born with a slight defect in his lip and mouth. He spoke little and when he did he often stuttered. From a young age the children mocked and beat on him. He would arrive home a physical and emotional mess. His older brother Allan wasn't the sharpest of boys and had trouble keeping a lid on his feelings. He was protective of Juan, coming to blows with anyone he caught picking on his younger brother," she said.

"We decided to homeschool them through middle school, hiring a nanny and a tutor," Marcus said. "Our home was large, with all the comforts. We thought that would provide them every convenience and advantage. They were the problem and we didn't do anything about it. When the first nanny told us the boys had discipline problems we blamed her and found a new one. This pattern persisted until we found staff that didn't complain about the boys. Where the boys were concerned we looked the other way."

"In time, we decided the boys needed the structure and discipline of a school environment. After they arrived home bloodied and bruised from fighting one afternoon, I sat them down explaining that they were Weeia. I said that they were better than all the children in that school combined. It was meant to boost their confidence. Plus, it was true, you know. I told them to fight back the next time someone picked on them, to fight back by any means necessary." She had the faraway look again. I supposed she was remembering the past.

"The boys began fighting back. They stopped coming home bruised and afraid. Instead they learned to intimidate the other children emotionally and physically to the point that school officials contacted us about their misbehavior," he said. "We didn't have any interest in curbing their conduct. After all they had been the victims for so long. We found out much later that by then, our youngest had gathered a group of the worst bullies around them to torment the other boys." He sounded proud of his children even though it seemed to me they had been cruel to others.

"By the time they began college Allan had shown Material abilities of great physical strength. When Juan began to develop as an Emotional henki, he discovered new better ways of entertaining himself. We figured he would eventually outgrow the habit as he matured. The problem was he liked to show off his abilities in front of humans." He looked at Marga who looked back with sad eyes.

"At first we paid little attention to the matter when The Elders notified us that Allen and Juan had violated the Moosehead Lake Agreement." I wondered what that was. The confusion must've shown on my face because Marga interrupted her husband to explain it to me.

"The Moosehead Lake Agreement was established many years ago in Maine. One of the most important terms of the agreement says that Weeia in North America, visitors and residents, are forbidden from revealing the existence of Weeia and our abilities to humans. The penalty is death."

"The thing is that we were busy buying out a competitor and traveling to Asia when the notices arrived. We thought it was no big deal and left it up to the boys to reply. Later, The Elders sent a summons." Again Marga stopped her husband to explain.

"A summons is when The Elders through a representative inform you that you are required to appear before them to answer questions. It's serious and not optional. We know that now. Back then we dismissed our friends concerns. The boys threw out the notices and forgot about the summons. We thought The Elders had better things to do than to monitor the behavior of college boys. We thought they would forget about the whole thing if we ignored it."

"We did the same thing with the two summons that

followed. In time, The Elders passed Judgment in Absentia. After they carried out the sentence they notified us that since Allan and Juan and we as their parents had been non responsive, the original reprimand to our sons had escalated to a death sentence."

"Your father, Thomas McKnight, as the enforcer of The Elders carried out the sentence." When Marga spoke her words were venomous. "He killed our boys." I didn't know what to say. I couldn't defend him. On the other hand, it seemed from what the Assugranes were telling me that my father was doing his job. While I didn't like the idea that he had killed two young men some might think of it as my father's duty to protect the Weeia.

"We couldn't believe what had happened. We looked for the boys in vain. Marcus found and confronted your father and he didn't deny carrying out the murders," she said in the same angry voice.

"He looked at me stoically, handed me the official Desist Order and walked away without a word of condolence or regret. He had taken our boys lives without a second thought, without feeling, without regard for our pain," Marcus said, an expression of pain crossing his face as he spoke.

I felt sorry for them. I couldn't imagine what it would be like to lose a child or in their case two children. There was an even sadder part of the story that they seemed to bypass even as they told me what happened. I got the clear impression neither Marga nor Marcus felt they had been at fault for teaching their children to take what they wanted from the world when it pleased them. Their children followed the example their parents set, believing that they were superior to humans and entitled to do as they desired without responsibility.

I hadn't met The Elders but from what I had heard about them their main role was to protect the Weeia. It occurred to me that the boys didn't know any better. Marga and Marcus should've disciplined them; but instead they thought their behavior was just a phase. It was easier to hate my father than to accept any blame for the results of their haphazard parenting.

If looks could kill Marga's would've pierced my heart at that moment. The anger seemed to bubble out of her and reach across the table to me. Her husband touched her hand with infinite gentleness and her stance softened. She dropped her eyes to the empty space between the cutlery in front of her. The raw grief and anguish that had been heavy in the air evaporated.

"Ready for your main course?" Before I had a chance to respond she signaled for Ping to bring our food. As I watched in silence Ping and Lala set a plate with an oversize grilled steak baked potatoes and broccoli in front of each of us. Marcus phone rang. He stepped away from the table to take the call, returning moments later with news that made Marga grin from ear to ear.

"That's wonderful that our friend has confirmed pick up of the goods as planned," she said after he whispered something in her ear.

They were downright jovial after that. I had lost my appetite. After two bites I abandoned my main course. Somehow I managed to sit through their small talk past dessert.

"Coffee or tea?" Marga asked me with the graciousness of a woman accustomed to entertaining guests.

"I can't eat another bite, thanks. I'll see you in the morning."

"Yes, of course." Marga said. "Some rest will do us all good."

"I'm sorry." I heard her say as I walked toward my room. I thought she might've been speaking to Marcus but when I turned back she was looking at me.

Ping and Lala arrived with tea at bedtime. There were so

many thoughts going through my head I was concerned I wouldn't be able to sleep. I realized that the red lights at the base of the floor were still an unknown, so I decided to sleep in the Cabana instead of my room that night. I crept across the trail to the waterside building where I fell into a deep sleep on the weather beaten couch.

Sometime late in the night I woke up to find someone in the Cabana with me. Although it was dark making it hard to see who was there I was able to distinguish that there were two people. That couldn't be good, I thought, remaining still. The next thing I knew one of them approached me. He, I thought it was a man, carried something that smelled of chemicals in his hand. The scent frightened me. I reached out with my mind for my father. I didn't think about the protective barrier the property was supposed to have that would keep my message from reaching him or whether my father would be awake at that hour to notice my call. Father help, was all I thought. Loud. Time must have slowed down because somehow in that instant I wondered how a silent mental call to my father could be loud.

As he reached down to cover my nose, I panicked. Fear, raw and visceral took over as he touched my face with the cloth. My face burned from the bite of the chemicals and my fear transformed into something different, anger. This place and these people had pushed me down again and again and this was the last straw. I wasn't going to take it anymore. I lashed out with everything I had in every direction before fading into darkness.

Chapter 17

A horrible pounding ache in my head woke me. In the instant I felt it, I wished I could return to the painless sleep. I remembered what had happened and wondered if it had been a bad dream. The pain said it wasn't. I was in a dark place which might be a good thing. Something told me I wouldn't welcome bright light. I didn't know how much time had passed or what had happened after the man had knocked me out.

It was a while, maybe two hours, before I heard any noise. It sounded like voices, none that I recognized. Deep ache and fatigue took over and I fell back asleep. When I woke the next time the hurt was less alive. There was a sliver of light coming through a thick curtain. A figure sat slumped on a chair next to my bed. As my eyes adjusted to the light I recognized Duncan and larger than life relief flooded me. If he was with me, everything must be okay.

He looked as tired as I felt and I didn't want to wake him. The need to go to the bathroom won over my hesitation driving me across the room to a door that stood ajar. I was thankful to still be wearing the long t-shirt I had gone to sleep in the night before. Was it the night before?

"The things women do to be pampered and get extra beauty sleep." A groggy voice greeted me on my return. Duncan, rubbing the cobwebs out of his eyes, was still in the chair.

"You look like you could use some beauty sleep yourself Speedy."

"That I could." He laughed.

"How are you feeling? The doctor said you would have a headache."

"I hadn't noticed." I tried for sarcasm and failed. "I feel

like something a camel chewed on and spat out."

"You must be feeling better if you're giving me lip."

"What could be better than camel spit? Speaking of such bright and cheerful subjects what happened? Last thing I remember there were two uninvited guests in the cabana, one of them was covering my nose. Then I woke up with the grandmother of all headaches here. Where's here? Where are we?"

"The way I heard the story nearly all the buildings on the property were destroyed before your father arrived. He killed the two masked men who were carrying you toward the gate. It seems their car was damaged by whatever destroyed the buildings. Do you know anything about that?"

"No, the last thing I remember two people dressed like thieves in all black attacked me in the night. I was afraid. My fear felt thick and strong. I called to my father before they knocked me out. Then I woke up here with you." As I looked around wondering what place we were in Duncan, as if reading my thoughts, responded to the question I had asked a minute earlier.

"In a large property about seven miles south of where Douglas Estate used to be. It looks like a well to do residential neighborhood."

"How long has it been? We need to go—" I had sat down on the bed while we chatted. As I began to get up I felt light headed. It seemed my body, which wanted no part of being upright, didn't share my enthusiasm about moving. It was all could do to keep the nausea down. I suspect if there had been any food in my stomach it would have come out. As it was I just doubled over.

"Easy there, tiger. It's better if you stay put until your head and your body make friends again." He held his arm out. I used it like a life preserver to keep me steady. A moment later the room stopped running in circles around me. Well, instead of running it jogged. I took advantage of the opportunity to sit down.

"You should rest until you feel better. It's obvious you can't get far in your current camel spit condition." That earned him what I imagined was a pathetic smile. If effort counted I deserved an "A" because it took all I had to manage the weakling facial expression.

"How about I find some lunch while you make yourself comfortable in that tiny bed of yours and when I return I'll fill you in on my newsworthy findings." I think I nodded agreement and watched him head for the door saying, "Be right back. Don't leave without me."

For the first time since I woke up I looked around at my surroundings. I was seated on the edge of a cushioned inviting king bed with a sea of pillows that beckoned me to slumber. Soft pale sheets topped by a matching duvet complimented the wall color and curtains. They weren't an exact match but it was so close I imagined an interior designer spending hours finding just the right ones. A pair of handsome night tables framed the bed which sat atop a thick wall to wall carpet that also matched the duvet, wall and curtain colors. There were two easy to reach reading lights above a cushioned headboard. A vanity took up one corner. A futon, where Duncan had been sitting a moment before, was on the opposite side of the room from the vanity. Judging by the impressions in the carpeting, it had been moved closer to the bed than its usual position.

The detailed inventory of the room helped me feel better. One small task at a time, I thought. I continued my observations to keep my mind distracted from the pounding pressure in my head and the waning desire to hurl. Central air conditioning kept the temperature constant. Although such comforts were ubiquitous in South Florida there had been no air conditioning in my previous accommodations making me notice them in my new ones. I wasn't sure if it was chilly or I was chilled. I longed to climb back under the covers. Recessed dimmer lights, I could see the switch on the wall from where I sat, were the final touch that convinced me we were in a nicer than average house. If the rest of the house was like the bedroom it was many times more modern and stylish than my former digs at Douglas Estate.

The sensation in my head had slowed down to a dull roar so I decided to chance it and stood up. Too sudden, the movement reminded me that I needed to take things easy for a bit longer. With great care and snail like movements I made my way to the side of the bed where I had been asleep just minutes earlier. I eased myself down into a sitting position, resting my back on a mound of pillows. I wasn't just sleepy. I was exhausted and felt ill. At the risk of falling asleep I closed my eyes. The room circled at a slower pace when my eyes were closed.

It seemed only seconds after I settled down that Duncan strolled in looking better for having had lunch or whatever meal it had been. I made a mental note to ask him.

"I'm not asleep Fastman." I managed, opening my eyes against my better judgment. "Spill. What's new since—" His cell phone silenced me. Keeping his conversation brief, he hung up and returned his attention back to me. I was pleased that my eyes were still open.

"I've been meaning to tell you about a couple of things." He began with a serious tone. "After we split up at Douglas Estate nine weeks ago, I put feelers out through my contacts at the Youth for Change group and everywhere I could think might lead to something, anything on who and why someone took a shot at you. The more I thought about it the more the shooting made no sense to me. It didn't seem like your father would've ordered someone to kill you when it would've been so easy for him to do it himself. He doesn't strike me as the squeamish type." He made a face.

"No, I suppose not." I managed to laugh. From the little I

knew of him, my father was many things, not all admirable, but squeamish wasn't one of them.

"There are too many rumors to count about your father and the ghoulish, terrible, and beyond belief things he's said to have done. He's the official enforcer for The Elders and that makes him, even if we discount the worst of the popular tales, a scary guy." He paused for effect and maybe even to make sure I was still awake. Even if had wanted to sleep by that point I was alert, listening to every word Duncan was saying. "The thing is, I found nothing, from a source I believe, that points to him ever killing a child, human or Weeia, not even a teenager without orders from The Elders. It's hard to explain why he'd kill you, his own daughter."

"I would not," my father's baritone voice said surprising us both. We had been so engrossed in our conversation we hadn't seen him standing at the half open bedroom door. "I have no reason to nor would I kill Amy. I know you distrust me and we will discuss that at the first opportunity. For now, I wish you to feel safe and know I will not harm you nor will I allow anyone else to do so." He directed his gaze at me. I was not feeling quite well enough for a confrontation. I nodded yes to let him know I appreciated his words.

"Or Duncan," I heard my voice before I realized the words had escaped as if of their own volition.

"Agreed." He said as an unexpected gentle smile appeared on his face making its way to his eyes. At that moment he looked charming and handsome. I could imagine how Mom had fallen in love with him in their youth. I felt my heart warm to him. "I see you are feeling better?" He looked at me, the uncertainty painted on his face somehow incongruous with the tough guy image I expected. I shrugged.

"She's a little gray around the gills," Duncan said gaining a puzzled expression from my father. "She's not yet ready to get up but the symptoms are passing." I couldn't have said it better myself, I thought.

As my father started turning I found my voice. "I'm well enough for conversation. Will you join us?" I pointed at a small chair in the corner guessing he wouldn't want to sit on the bed. If he'd known how woozy I still was I imagine he wouldn't have taken the seat. I was too curious to give it another thought. Before he had a chance to change his mind about staying I badgered him with questions about what had happened at Douglas Estate.

After a moment he said "I am not certain what happened, Amy. In the deep hours of the predawn I woke to your urgent cry. It is fortunate that I am a light sleeper or I might have slept through your single feeble call through our bond." I was remembering the details now. It happened so fast. At first, I fought my attackers, kicking and flailing. The second person (I didn't know if it was a man or a woman) pressed down hard on my legs until I could no longer move them. The man held my arms to keep me from defending myself. I remembered the chemical smell on the cloth. Desperate and not knowing what else to do, I called my father in my mind. It was almost a reflex. Then everything went black.

"Do you remember what happened before you called me?"

"I didn't until now." I described what had happened.

"Do you know who they were? Had you seen them before?" I moved my head sideways.

It occurred to me he must know something more. "Do you?"

"I do not know your attackers. The owners of the property are old enemies. I had no idea they owned property in Miami let alone that you were their guest." He looked at me, a question in his eyes.

"I only met the Assugranes last night. When I returned at the end of the day they were there. After a very odd meal with the two of them, it was clear to me that they weren't dealing from a full deck. Apparently they blame you for the death of their sons?" I wondered if he knew how they had shifted responsibility for their own failings onto my father. I let the question hang and watched his reaction.

"I know what they blame me for, but it was their fault for ignoring the sanctions from The Elders." My father's eyes blazed with anger.

"They offered us shelter after someone took a shot at me the day after you and I met. I already told you that story. They also offered a Weeia trainer who would help me develop my abilities. Mom and I (I thought it best to leave Duncan out of the conversation for his own benefit) decided to accept until we found another solution. It was when we met with them on our way into the property that there was an explosion and Mom was hurt."

It was true that it was a joint decision. Since I could remember Mom had always involved Kat and me in important decisions. We always had a say. We had grown closer since the two of us had been on the run together, after being separated from Kat. I felt my heart squeezed by invisible hands that made me worry and ache for Mom.

"It was through friends of my parents that I made the connection. They're pillars of their community. I should've asked more questions but we had little time. We were so afraid someone would try to kill Amy again and we didn't know how they had found her in the first place. We were afraid we couldn't keep her safe." Duncan's voice was laced with traces of the anxiety we had felt all those weeks before. "Ever since I saw Amy again I've been worried about her. Now that she's out of that place I realize something was very wrong."

"Did they know you were my daughter when they invited you to stay there?" My father asked.

"They knew last night. Knowing what we do now, they must have known from the start. The Assugranes weren't there when we arrived. Other than the security guards who didn't seem to know anything much about the property goings on, I only ever saw three staff, Master Zhao Tse, Ping and Lala. The only one who spoke English was Master Tse and he didn't say much. He was always blowing me off about the abilities training and telling me to meditate."

My father asked about my life at Douglas Estate. As I described my daily routine and minimal meals he became angry. By then I was feeling better. I told them about the lights in my bedroom. I explained my suspicions about the bedtime tea being drugged and how I thought they were poisoning me. I didn't explain that I had been able to dreamshift the tea while awake, unsure of what that might mean regarding my abilities.

"They knew the names Amy and Barbara but the last name Barbara gave wasn't McKnight," Duncan offered.

"I am not sure it would matter. My enemies are well informed. They know my wife's name. They must know I have a daughter." My father's voice was harsh. "I do not yet know how they knew your whereabouts."

"You think your enemies knew who we are and that's why they offered us a place to stay?" That would go a long way toward explaining many odd things about my stay at the property.

"Yes." My father said.

"I couldn't figure out why they would invite us there then treat us, me, like a guest who has overstayed her welcome." I hadn't thought about it in so many words while I was at Douglas Estate. Feeling I had no choice, but to stay there for my own safety I had forced myself to put up with the unpleasantness of life there. I believed if I left the property there was a good chance I might be killed. Now I realized I was living at my father's enemy's property all along. "Now, it's clear that I was an unwanted guest. When I discovered the tea was drugged I began to work on a plan to escape. The problem is that by then I wasn't feeling well."

"You were more than an unwanted guest. You were a bargaining chip. If that failed you were a way to exact revenge on me." His harsh voice was back.

"It fits," Duncan added, a serious expression on his face. "I had begun to suspect that the shot at you was because you're his daughter. Knowing about Douglas Estate makes it the right explanation. Somehow your father's enemies found you. Maybe it was the same way we met. If you remember I was following McKnight." I was not sure how my father would react to the news that he'd led his enemies to me. I was not thrilled to be the center of attention of my father's enemies. On the other hand, I was relieved to know what was going on.

"You mean I was shot at, almost blown up, mistreated for weeks and attacked in bed to get at my father?" I looked at Duncan who nodded. My father agreed, saying "I believe your friend is correct."

That seemed too easy. Why was my father, the baddie enforcer, sitting here with us instead of out there getting back at his enemies? "What happened yesterday?"

"It is still confusing Amy. When I realized it was you calling me, I jumped right to you and found myself in the middle of chaos. By the time I made my way dreamshifting around the large estate all the buildings had imploded and the entire place was choked with smoke and dust. I found two mercenaries dragging you unconscious towards the gate and neutralized them. That bought me time to drive over and pick you up to transfer you here before the police found you."

"I almost took you to the hospital. I do not know what they used to drug you. It was powerful and you did not look well. If you had not snapped out of it as you did I would have moved you to the emergency room, but I was concerned about leaving you and your mother unprotected at the hospital while I was away. I did not have security staff with me. I did not know how to contact Duncan."

"By neutralize you mean kill, don't you?"

"Yes. There is no point in telling you otherwise. That is who I am. That is what I do when necessary. But I was not the one that collapsed the buildings and destroyed the compound; someone or something else took care of that." I didn't know what to believe. There was no reason for him to lie.

"After you left me here you found your enemies didn't you?"

"If you mean Marcus and Marga Assugranes, I know where they are indeed. I will be away for a few days to deal with that threat to you, your sister, if they know where she is, and your mother." I felt a twinge of pity for them all. They had attacked us even though we had never done anything to them and didn't even know who they were. "They are too afraid to confront me so they attack my family. They are cowards." There was deep anger and a healthy dose of frustration in my father's voice. From the little I knew about my father I suspected we disagreed on many things. Today, I was glad we agreed on this.

"What twisted, twisted people to have offered help when they meant harm." Duncan spoke the words I was thinking.

"I have made enemies over the years. There are many others who wish me and my family ill. When I heard Amy describe a letter that fooled her, it narrowed the field considerably. Only a few know how to construct such objects." My father stood up.

"There will be more threats I am afraid. If word gets out that the Assugranes attacked my family without repercussions others will follow soon. I must attend to this right away Amy before we can help your mother. It would be good to warn your sister. Do you know where she lives?"

"We were separated when Mom and I were kidnapped last year. I wish I knew where she is."

"That may be for the best. If we cannot find her perhaps my enemies will not find her either."

While I saw the logic in his thinking a twinge of worry assaulted me. I hoped she was safe and well wherever she was. "Can you use your bond with her like you did to find me?"

"I do not have such a bond with her, perhaps her abilities are different from ours. I have engaged the services of a full-time housekeeper to look after you while I am out of town. Her name is Marcia Martinez. She's from the Dominican Republic. She speaks Spanish and only a few words of English. She can understand English if you speak slowly. She will clean, cook, do laundry and anything you need. There is food in the kitchen." I thought it was considerate of my father to look at Duncan when he said that. Then he turned to me. I thought for a moment he was going to hug me. Instead he said, "If you need anything ask Mrs. Martinez."

I felt afraid that he was leaving, in part because there might be killers looking for me and in part because he might put himself in harm's way. I wasn't comfortable calling him dad and McKnight didn't fit either. "Father, how do I reach you if something happens?" I didn't want to say if someone else attacks me while I'm sleeping or if I'm worried about you.

He turned to me. "You have but to think of me, as you did last night, and I will hear you. If you prefer you may call my cell phone. I gave the number to Mr. Bittersdorp. Do not be afraid, Amy. Your friend has offered to stay as long necessary. He will watch over you while you sleep. I have guards posted around the property. This house will be safe from intruders, of that you can be sure."

"What about you?" We might not have a close father daughter relationship but I didn't wish him dead. Besides I needed him. My father looked tired and stressed.

"I will be fine. I will return as soon as possible." Without another word he walked out. I thought of getting up and going after him. It was not a good idea. I was so tired and my head hurt. If he realized how I felt he might want me to go to the hospital.

Chapter 18

I felt sad and worried to see him go. There were things about my father I didn't like and didn't approve of but he was still my father. On the plus side, we had just reconnected after what seemed like such a long time. And, he'd agreed to do something risky and selfless to try to bring back Mom. Score one for the good guys, I thought. I crossed my fingers that he'd return safe to me. There was nothing else I could do.

At the moment, getting out of bed was a huge accomplishment. My head was still hurting and I felt tired and nauseous. Duncan's look of concern didn't match the light tone in his voice when he suggested I sleep.

"Get some rest camel spit girl. I'll check on you in a little while and we can continue our conversation."

The next thing I knew I woke up from a dream. I was sweating buckets and it felt like my head was splitting in two. I focused on slowing my breathing and sometime later, I don't know how long, I began feeling better. The splitting became throbbing, an improvement. After a while I felt well enough to get up. A thoughtful person, maybe the housekeeper, had left a new toothbrush and a change of clothes for me. I had been wearing the same outfit, almost every day, for weeks. It would feel like such a luxury to brush my teeth and wear something else after I cleaned up.

The shower left me invigorated and tired at the same time. A look out my window revealed night had fallen. Sporting clean teeth, my new found clothes and a pair of fluffy house slippers I found at the foot of my bed I went in search of Duncan. I figured he wouldn't be far. If I knew Duncan at all, chances were good he'd be in or near the kitchen.

A couple of turns through dark hallways and unoccupied rooms led me to a large kitchen with a single occupant.

"Amy, it's great to see you join the living again." I must look better, I thought, since his face matched his tone. "Would her ladyship join me at the dining table for a spot of food?"

I hadn't thought about eating until he spoke. I noticed several pots atop the stove. The varied smells of home cooked food made me salivate and I realized I was hungry. "Yes, I would. What have you got Speedy? Is there enough for both of us? What about Mrs. Martinez, did she have dinner already?"

"She's gone for the day. She said she'd be back in time for breakfast. She cooked up a storm before leaving. There's enough food for a small army. Even I won't be able to eat everything Mrs. Martinez made." His wink told me not to believe what he said. "She made tasty shredded beef, white rice, kidney beans, fried plantains, a large salad, oh, and two types of dessert since she wasn't sure which one you might like. There's also fresh Cuban and French bread. The refrigerator is bursting and there's every variety of fruit known to man in several bowls on the kitchen counter."

"I'll start with some salad and work my way up to the hot dishes. Did you eat already?"

"I snacked a bit. I can't tell a lie." He gave me a mischievous smile.

"I've seen you 'snack a bit' and it's like two meals for a regular person." He laughed.

"Well I saved my main appetite in case you woke hungry we could enjoy dinner together." It was my turn to laugh.

"Good to know you have a main appetite. I thought it was all a main appetite Fastman."

"Naw, camel spit girl. You're just envious because I can eat more than you." It was a sign of how much better I looked that he was teasing me.

"I'll neither confirm nor deny such rumors."

Between the two of us we warmed up the food and served

up a feast. It was wonderful to eat a homemade meal. If I discounted the soups that passed for meals at Douglas Estate it had been a while since I had had one. And, sharing it with Duncan made it that much more special. As we neared dessert, Duncan turned serious again.

"Amy, the other thing I had been about to tell you earlier was that I did some digging. I checked with a couple of older Weeia and several sources. It seems Unelmoija is a half mythical or historical figure depending on which version you choose to believe. Oo-nehl-moh-ee-ah is how most of them pronounced the word. There's no universal agreement but it's probable Unelmoija is or was female."

"Is or was?" I asked, a bit puzzled by the strange wording.

"That's the odd part, one source referred to her as a historical character from the distant past, and the others seem to think she's coming. The stories are inconsistent and contradictory. Three of my sources say she's due to come in the future, so I'll assume that's the more accurate story." It sounded like a bunch of hogwash to me. What I couldn't fathom was where the psychic had come up with a Weeia fairytale.

"Some fear she'll bring about the destruction of our people. Others hope she'll be the bringer of a better, freer way of life. Some believe major changes will follow her arrival." His words reminded me of what the psychic had said. She'd looked puzzled when she spoke as if she didn't understand everything she was telling me. I hadn't picked up on that until I realized that she might not be Weeia.

"That's similar to what the psychic told me. Do you think she's Weeia?"

"Who, the psychic?" I nodded.

"No, I didn't get the impression that she was."

"Is there a way to know for sure if someone is Weeia?"

"Other than that person telling you, it's difficult to spot Weeia. A few powerful Weeia have the ability to identify other Weeia when they use their abilities. There are rumors that The Elders have a dedicated person whose job it is to keep tabs on the location of each Weeia. They're said to have detailed books on Weeia people, their abilities and power level. Most Weeia, unless they're afraid for some reason, are happy to say hello when they run into a fellow Weeia. I don't know for sure. She seemed like a regular human to me."

"What do you mean power level?"

"Most of our people are Lowes in terms of their power. They may have a strong sensitivity to food, wine, colors and so forth but they can't alter anything with their abilities. That's the lowest level of power. Others, like me, are Medius or medium level. Our abilities require medium energy. A few among the Weeia can change things. They're Maximus or high level. That means their power is strong and they can change things. The most powerful Weeia, The Elders, are Maximus. Your father, for example, is strong and can change things. He can project himself into a lifelike image, command or even kill at will."

"So what power Weeia am I?" I didn't think about the answer when I blurted out the question.

"I don't know for sure— but— I think you're Medius like me."

"Why do you think that?"

"You're a dreamshifter, but not a very powerful one compared to the others I've heard of in stories— and you have a bond that allows you to communicate with your father without electronics. Maybe you will become more powerful, it's all very personal."

I thought what he said made sense. "Going back to the Unelmoija thing, I wonder where the psychic got that from if she's not Weeia. Even more important, why did she think I have anything to do with Unelmoija when I had never heard of her, it, whatever until she mentioned it?"

"I dunno." Duncan looked as puzzled as I felt.

"What else did you find out about Unelmoija? When is it supposed to arrive? Like, what year?"

"Nobody seems to know."

"How will Weeia know he or she is the Unelmoija? Or perhaps there are several Unelmoija?"

"I think there's only one. The thing everyone I spoke with shared was deep respect for the Unelmoija."

"Why respect?"

"Because of how profound they think Unelmoija will be in the lives of Weeia, how she's expected to change our lives." He had a distant look on his face.

"What do you mean? What will she do?"

"Nobody seems to know exactly. It may be that we will know it when the time comes. Whatever it is believers are convinced her arrival will spark major changes among us."

"How will we know someone is the Unelmoija?"

"Good question. Of course there's controversy around that too. The consensus is that she'll have all of our abilities."

"So that psychic must have me confused with someone else."

"Maybe you will develop more abilities, you're still young."

"In that case, you may address me as Your Highness and I shall knight you Sir Duncan." I couldn't stop giggling, it was so ridiculous. Duncan burst into laughter and then we both laughed together. One of us would stop and then the other would start. It was a while before we calmed down.

"We needed a good laugh. All the tension and worry found a healthy way out." Duncan, back to normal, said looking like there was more on his mind.

"That was fun."

"There's more, Amy. Believers say she'll be one of the most powerful Weeia ever to exist." He stopped, turning serious. "Many welcome the arrival of Unelmoija. A few believe Unelmoija will be our downfall and have sworn to destroy her as soon as she appears."

"Why are you so serious? That psychic just made a mistake; I don't fit the description of Unelmoija at all."

"I'm worried about that psychic labeling you Unelmoija. Did you mention that to anyone other than your mum?"

I shook my head from side to side to let him know I hadn't. "Who would believe that about me anyway?"

"It doesn't matter if you believe you're Unelmoija or if you use your abilities. It doesn't even matter how good you are at using them. If a rumor starts, if someone else hears about it and believes it they might try to kill you. Even if they know nothing about you, even if they don't believe it's true they may not want to take any chances. There are some crazy people out there. We have recent proof of what crazy people are capable of doing."

He made a scary face and wiggled his hands in the air. This won him a brief viewing of my tongue stuck out in mock reply.

"Even among Weeia there are fanatics looking for a cause to rally." He kept talking while I cleared the table and he brought out dessert plates.

"We already have one killer after you because of your father. I say we avoid another because of this mystical character. Don't ya think?" The funny voice lightened the tone of the topic. I nodded in agreement moving on to a more pressing topic, dessert.

"Yum."

"I agree."

"Which one do you like better?"

"What's this?" I pointed to the white topped sinful piece of heaven on my plate.

"Tres leches."

"What you said. Though I might collapse into a diabetic coma if I have any more."

"You diabetic?"

"Naw, just something I heard somewhere."

"Tomorrow is another day and you can watch your figure or whatever it is that girls do. Today, I say you eat like it's the last day and toss your worries aside."

"Sounds good to me." My head still hurt though I felt much better. The shower, dinner, laughter and conversation had been the best medicine. I must have looked thoughtful because Duncan asked how I was feeling.

"Like a million bucks." I fibbed. I felt more like a million bucks that had been depreciated down to five bucks. I cut off a small slice of the decadent milky dessert. A part of me felt like I had to eat while there was food available. I was no longer at Douglas Estate and the property had been destroyed but my memories lingered like ghosts.

"You up for a movie?" I welcomed the change of topic.

"What you got?"

"There's a DVD player with a bunch of old movies and a fast internet connection so we can stream movies too. How about a science fiction movie where they travel to the stars or the one where they rescue the whales?"

"Don't know either one. Whichever has the happiest ending." I couldn't handle a tear jerker. Plus I still felt tired and groggy even though I had slept more hours than I wanted to count. It was not like me to be so— Duncan interrupted my thoughts to point to a seat in front of the large flat screen television.

"You sit right here. I'll put away the leftovers and tidy the kitchen. Your Highness can just lift her royal feet up and make interesting conversation." Any other day I'd have marched to the kitchen and helped; that night I just wanted to curl under a blanket and relax. I tended to sleep well and wake up full of energy. This listless teenager was not me.

"I'll do my best at interesting conversation. You're welcome to pick any movie as long as it has a happy-ish ending."

I must have fallen asleep. I woke to find Duncan watching a science fiction movie. He insisted on escorting me back to my room.

"The fluffy girly bed is yours. The masculine futon is mine. Keep off." His fake warning made me smile. "I'll be back in a few minutes."

I opened my mouth to tell him there was no need to watch over me and decided I'd sleep better knowing he was near. "As if I'd want anything to do with your forest green futon Fastman. I have soft girly sheets."

I woke up startled out of a deep slumber, my heart racing. As I sat up in the bed I felt sweat pouring down my face, back and chest. I must have mumbled in my sleep or said something when I woke because Duncan was watching me.

"I didn't think the end of the movie was bad enough to give you nightmares." He tried for funny. I didn't have the energy to remember what movie it had been and was too frazzled to care. My head hurt and I felt nauseous again. I must have been a sight because concern showed on his face. I was thankful that he waited a few minutes.

"You don't look well and I'm getting worried Amy. What's wrong?" I explained in as few words as I could muster how I felt.

"You don't seem surprised. Has this happened a lot?" I was expecting him to ask for details and was unprepared for his question.

"Second time. First time yester ... day."

"That explains why you looked like something from a zombie flick when you showed up in the kitchen. I take it that's what you mean by yesterday?" My throbbing head was not happy when I nodded yes.

"Any idea what brought this on?"

I suspected moving my head from side to side wouldn't feel any better than moving it up and down had so I mumbled no.

"Hmm. It must be related to what they used to knock you out or something they gave you after that."

"Does it hurt anywhere?"

Duh. I was sore everywhere, tired too. Oh yeah, and I wanted to detach my head from my body. I made a face.

"I mean do you have any places that feel like more than bruising or general achiness?"

Now that he mentioned it, the back of my neck had a sore spot. After a few minutes, the speed the room circled at dropped. As soon as I felt I was not about to lose dinner to the carpet I motioned to the back of my neck. Duncan moved closer.

"I'm going to turn on the light, 'kay?" He must have assumed my lack of reply meant yes because moments later he switched the night lamp on and drew it close to me. I leaned forward and moved my hair out of the way.

"There's a puncture wound there." He pressed down. "Does that hurt?" I yelped in reply.

"I'll take that as a yes."

"How long has that been there?" I shrugged my shoulders. At least that didn't make my head throb more or make the room spin faster.

Although I wasn't glad the staff had died the night I was attacked I didn't feel a sense of loss. They hadn't been kind to me. Worse yet the more I thought about it the more it became obvious that they hurt me on purpose while I was in their care.

Chapter 19

I was restless that night, sleeping in fits and starts. I noticed a pattern of sorts. Every time I began to dream I became anxious and woke up. When I did, Duncan was there watching over me, concern marring his face.

Close to dawn I saw that Duncan had dozed off. I felt bad thinking he must have been exhausted and sleepy after keeping an eye on me all night. Instead of lying back down I sat up and meditated. Meditation always calmed me. I had taught myself a way to go from serene meditation to dreamshifting. I wasn't awake and I wasn't asleep. I was in the middle. It had taken me months to learn how to do it. That was how I had found Mom at the hospital, using the meditation to dreamshifting path. Now that I thought about it at least I had learned something useful during my time at Douglas Estate even if I had to learn on my own and in spite of the interference from Master Tse.

Moments after I began to dreamshift I felt pressure in my head, then my heartbeat increased and my pulse raced. A slow headache spread like a bright color splash in clear water until every corner of my head throbbed. As the dream ended the nausea began. A soft gasp escaped my lips and I thought for sure it would wake Duncan.

When I turned to check he was fast asleep. I didn't blame him. That was what reasonable people did at that uncivilized hour, as my mother would say. I envied him his deep slumber.

I felt restless and tired at the same time. I pondered getting up to settle the feeling one way or the other. Instead, for Duncan's sake, I stayed in bed. I was sure if I got up I'd wake him up. I managed to rest a few hours longer.

The secret was not to dreamshift. The mental exercise had

been painful but worthwhile. At least I knew what was giving me the horrible headaches. Under normal circumstances I wouldn't care too much, but I had to rely on my ability to get Mom out of her coma. It might be the only way to bring her back. I had to find a way to dreamshift without the new debilitating side effects. But how?

"Get any sleep?" Duncan's voice, sounding as groggy as I felt, broke into my thoughts.

"Some. You?"

"Slept like a baby." He was not fooling me. I knew he'd been awake the better part of the night. It was sweet of him to make light of it so I wouldn't feel worse than I did. I was lucky to have such a good friend.

I should go for a jog but I couldn't muster the energy. As if he knew what I was thinking Duncan said, "You jogging?" It was not surprising that he'd ask since we had met on one of my morning runs. It was nice of him to think about it.

"Not today." I hated to skip another morning. Maybe I'd do some stretching instead.

"How about a swim?"

"Great idea. Is there a pool?"

"Yep, the house comes complete with housekeeper, security staff and large swimming pool. Oh, and it's on a canal. The realtor showed me around while you were counting sheep yesterday."

"There's only one problem."

"What? It's a nice house. You might as well take advantage of it."

"There's just one detail missing. What do you need to take advantage of the pool Fastman?"

"Um, the will to swim? Some lazy bones young woman just seems to want to lounge in bed all day." I threw a pillow at him.

"It's only seven a.m. Fastman." An early morning swim would be fun. "I don't have anything to wear in the pool. Do you?"

"This is a nudist neighborhood." He winked at me.

"Very funny. You go first and show me how it's done."

"I'm too modest to swim nekked on my own. We'll have to find something to wear in the pool. I know a type of costume was invented for use in swimming pools and at the beach, about one hundred years ago."

"You're so well informed." I batted my eyelashes at him. "What would I do without the benefit of your knowledge?" More exaggerated batting earned me a reply with a smile.

"That I am littl' lady. That I am."

"Who's that supposed to be?"

"A famous cowboy actor you're too young to know about. I'm glad a little humor has returned some color to your cheeks. I see what you mean. Let's grab some breakfast, I'm starving. When the stores open later we can buy some of those special clothes you insist on wearing in the pool."

The headache and its friends lethargy and nausea didn't agree with food in general. I'd have been content with fruit and cereal just to have something in my tummy.

Duncan had other plans. Pancakes with real maple syrup, scrambled eggs with ham and cheese, toast, bacon, fruit and cereal were on that morning's menu. In part because everything smelled and tasted better than good, and in part because Duncan was convinced that he was going to force whatever ills I had out and replace them with food, I ate more than I meant to when we sat down.

After breakfast, Duncan insisted we call my father. I had had enough of the spooky mind communications so we used a good old fashioned telephone. Given his dislike for cell phones we thought to reach him at his hotel room first. I assumed Duncan would want me to call and was surprised to see him dial. The hotel answered and forwarded the line to the requested room. It rang a few times and I heard someone pick up.

"McKnight?" Straight to the point without so much as a greeting. "She was drugged. Last night, we found a puncture wound on the back of her neck. She's not sure how long it's been there but she doesn't remember her neck feeling sore before the night of the attack. That's probably what's making her sick. Maybe it's an allergic reaction." Duncan listened to my father, mumbling agreement every so often then saying he'd take me before hanging up.

"What did he say? What do you mean you'll take me? Where?" I didn't like being left out of the conversation and said so.

"Calm yourself young woman. Your father suggested a blood test to find out what they injected in your neck. That seems like a good idea, no?" I said nothing waiting for him to tell me the rest. "There's a trustworthy lab in Miami near Bethel, the public hospital. It's hard to get an appointment the same day except your father can get in anytime. You want to know too, don't you?"

"Yes," I grumbled begrudgingly.

"Okay then. It's across town so it will take a while to get there. After the lab we can go shopping. Deal?"

"Mmhm."

"Oh, and we're not supposed to tell them he's your father so watch what you say. In fact, the less you say the better around those people. There are bound to be gossips there. The less they know the safer it'll be for you."

There was a car in the driveway. Duncan got behind the wheel as if it was his. I noticed he had to adjust the seat and mirrors.

"Whose car is this Fastman?"

"How do you know it's not mine?"

"'Cause I got eyes. Spill."

"Your dad—"

"He's not my dad. He's my father. Those are two different things."

"Okay, okay don't get your knickers in a twist. As I was saying when I was interrupted, your father left it for us to use. I hadn't decided whether to accept, thinking we could get around without it but the lab is across town and not in the best of areas. The car is here already. It'll be safer and faster. You good?"

"Yeah, alright." I wasn't happy about it but it made sense.

After downloading directions to the lab we set off. I wanted to learn more about Miami, a sprawling narrow urban area hugging the southeast coast of Florida. I had spent almost a year there and had seen little of the city. If I understood well, there were more than forty municipalities within what was called Miami by most visitors. Many of the streets running north and south changed names as they entered each municipality. For example, Flagler Street or U.S. Route 1 divided east from west, changing names as it flowed north up to Palm Beach and beyond. Each municipality had its own dividing line like Miami Avenue to separate north and south. Every one of them seemed to have their own version of Ocean Avenue.

We were staying in Pinecrest. By looking at the position of the sun relative to where I was I was able to figure out my general direction and find my way around. Sometimes it was confusing, like when a municipality changed the names of streets that crossed it, or didn't make sense. That was the case with Pinecrest, a residential neighborhood with a southwest address although it was in the southeast of the city. The lab address made more sense. It had a northwest address and it was north and west of us a fair bit. To get there we had to hop on U.S. Route 1, a busy multi-lane road, to connect onto Interstate 95, the city's main north south highway. It would lead us north to the lab.

Nothing to it except for slow traffic sprinkled with aggressive and rude drivers for good measure. Miami was known as home to some of the worst drivers in the nation.

Duncan didn't say anything more about the lab and I didn't ask. We turned the radio on in the car and lost ourselves to our thoughts. As we neared the exit I returned my attention to the task at hand and became curious about our destination and errand.

"Will they need my ID? I just realized I don't have any. The few things I had were at Douglas Estate. What about money? I have some but if it's expensive—"

"Not to worry Amy. Once we say your father sent us, I doubt they will need any kind of identification or money. He'll have made arrangements. If for some reason they ask for money, I have some on me. It should be enough. Although if it's expensive we may have to give up shopping."

I half punched him in the arm. "No can do. We can give up lunch which, if I know you at all, you're planning already. Let's see, shopping or food, food or shopping." I held my hands in the air weighing the two against each other in an invisible scale. "For sure, shopping beats food."

"Oh, how you wound me." He scrunched his face as if in pain. "Food is the essence of life and it provides the energy I need to survive. Would you deprive me?"

"It's not like we're walking to the lab Fastman. You ate enough breakfast for four people. I'm sure you can survive until we return home. You just like to sample exotic foods and Miami has exotic foods in every other corner."

"That's one of the things I like most about this subtropical city."

"I bet you already have a place in mind for lunch, don't you?"

"Not yet but I have some interesting ideas. I'm not familiar with this part of town. I thought I would search online when we arrived at the lab." His eyes lit up with glee at the thought. "You're a tough customer. Lunch and swimsuits it is."

Chapter 20

Parking was hard to find. After circling around the lab building searching several times we noticed a gated section in the back with ample parking space. An attendant sat in the shade looking unhappy. Putting my best face on I walked over to him and asked how much it cost to park there. He answered "Noh espeake de English. Dis praheevaht pahrkeeng. Goh away."

I was about to insist when a woman I hadn't noticed before approached me from across the parking lot. She had short hair the color of straw, gray blue eyes, and the kind of pale skin seen on people who spend all their time indoors. A faded cartoon mouse looked out from a black t-shirt which covered her pear shaped figure. She looked middle aged. Past fifty, I thought. Faded white sports shoes with socks and Bermuda shorts covered the lower half of her body. A leash hung from her hand leading to a beagle with a pink collar who stood at her feet as if waiting for something to happen.

At first glance she looked ordinary, dull even. As she drew closer to me, I noticed a kind of energy surrounded her. It was more something I could feel rather than see. It reminded me of the sensation I had felt when Duncan and I first met. My mother and father vibrated with energy too. This was different though I was unable to explain how.

"Who are you?" She blurted as soon as she was close enough to speak without shouting. I thought the question was odd but there seemed no harm in answering.

"I'm Amy. What's your name? Do you work here?" She looked at me for so long I thought she wasn't going to answer.

"I'm Jennifer, the manager of Tech Labtron. This lot is for

our VIP customers. No exceptions. If you're looking for parking I suggest you try seventh avenue about six blocks away and walk back." I remembered that was the name of the place where we were going. They weren't much on the welcome department.

"Oh, okay, thanks."

Thirty minutes later we made our way to the Tech Labtron building. The area around the building was more crowded than when we had first arrived. Instead of using the elevator we walked up the stairs following the signs to the main entrance. I was unprepared for the sea of people that took up every single seat and corner of the arrival room. Duncan pressed forward toward the reception desk. A heavyset woman wearing a wig sat behind the counter. She was talking on the phone and looking at her computer screen. When she hung up she ignored us, looking down at the sign-in sheet and calling a name out loud.

"Miss." Duncan's words were loud enough for her to hear them. She continued to show no sign that she was aware we were there.

"Miss, excuse me. We have an appointment." This time there was authority in his voice. She looked up.

"Ain't nobody got an appointment." Her tone was sharp. She looked disinterested.

"Ask your supervisor if Mr. Marcus Arvis called for an appointment. We were informed we would be seen right away." Looking incredulous she dialed an extension on her phone and asked about the appointment. She hung up without a word. Then turned to Duncan "Wait here."

A moment passed before a man opened the door beside the reception desk. Looking apologetic he introduced himself and led us into the interior of the office.

We followed him through fluorescent white hallways turning left and right until we reached a spartan office with a desk facing two empty chairs. As we sat down he spoke in a hurried voice. "I'm so sorry. I was expecting you later. I hadn't told the receptionist you were coming. I hope you didn't have to wait long. My boss told me to take care of you right away. How can I help you?"

"We need a Full Spectrum Rainbow blood analysis."

"I see. Just a moment please." He picked up the phone and spoke to someone else. "I have a Full Spectrum Rainbow client in my office. That's your area. No, no— I'll walk them over myself. This is a VIP request from the top."

I smiled when I saw Jennifer sitting behind a desk in a messy office that was the complete opposite of the one we had come from a moment earlier. She was sporting a white lab coat over a pale blue dress. The beagle was nowhere in sight. She must have heard our footsteps because she looked up. Recognition blossomed on her face as we arrived. For a moment she said nothing. She just stared at me. Then, as if shaking off a vision, she rose to her feet and invited us to have a seat. The sensation I had felt when we met returned as soon as I sat down across from her.

"Hello again. I didn't know who you were or I would've invited you to park in the VIP lot." She looked at me, curiosity crowding her face. I smiled. "I understand you requested a Full Spectrum Rainbow analysis?" There was uncertainty in her voice as she turned to Duncan. "Is it for you both?"

He looked so serious, I was tempted to break the mood but didn't think he would appreciate it at that moment. "It's just for her. We'll follow standard observation protocols. I was told you can process it today." He looked up in search of confirmation.

"Yes, of course. Anything else?"

"That's the only test we require. Was payment settled?"

"Yes. There's nothing for you to worry about. Follow me please." We walked behind Jennifer further down the fluorescent white hallways and deeper into the building. As we turned a corner, we found a set of closed double metal doors. Jennifer lifted the ID badge that hung from her neck and ran it through the electronic scanner to the right of the door until the red light turned to green. She punched in a long code into a number pad before pressing her thumb onto the same pad. I heard a soft click before she pulled open one of the doors that blocked our way.

We walked in silence for a couple of minutes until we reached a spacious room with a single occupant. Large complex looking machines in multiple sizes, colors and shapes lined the walls next to several gray metal cabinets. Test tubes, beakers, pipettes, microscopes and all manner of lab equipment sat atop the counters. In a corner of the bright lit room was a mousy looking woman, half standing, and half sitting on a tall stool. The noise from her equipment must've drowned out our arrival or else she was concentrating on something important because she didn't look up when we entered the room. Jennifer stopped partway into the room and waited. While we stood next to her I looked at our surroundings and at the woman.

Her shoulder length hair hung down shape free and disheveled. Large framed glasses were the main attraction on her emotionless face. She was thin, almost gaunt. A white lab coat hung over her clothes, covering faded blue jeans and a blue t-shirt. She wore brown clogs over light brown socks. I didn't blame her for the socks. It was cold inside the building. I figured low temperatures were necessary for a lab environment. After a few minutes Jennifer cleared her throat several times until the woman looked at her. Irritation appeared on her face. She didn't hide it.

"Mara, per Dr. Erdhal you're to drop whatever you're working on. These people are VIPs." Jennifer watched Mara as if to make sure what she said was registering. Mara continued what she was doing. Jennifer repeated the words a little louder. This time Mara looked at Jennifer when she spoke. She tensed. Her irritation seemed to worsen at the mention of Dr. Erdhal.

"Fine, what's so urgent?"

"You're to perform a Full Spectrum Rainbow analysis with standard observation protocols right now. Are you able to do that or do I need to call someone in?"

"I'll do it. Both of them?" She looked at us for the first time.

"Just on the woman. I'll monitor your progress as soon as I return from the hospital. Are you sure you're up to it?"

"Yes, just get on with it so I can start the tests. The sooner I finish that the sooner I can return to my work."

"Call me if you run into any trouble." And, she was gone.

As soon as Jennifer left Mara relaxed, a lot. "What's got into her? Are you the President's daughter or something?" She laughed at her own joke as I shook my head from side to side.

"This is gonna take a while. You might want to go to the bathroom if you're going to watch the whole thing. First door down the hall on the right." I looked at Duncan and he nodded.

When I returned they were chatting. Mara's whole body language had changed. She was smiling.

"It's kind of exciting. I haven't done a Full Rainbow in a long time. They're expensive you know. Only a few labs still offer them." Somewhere between when I left and when I returned Mara had become best buds with Duncan, to hear her side of the conversation.

"I always wanted to study to be a lab tech but my grandfather would have none of it. I'm excited to watch today."

"I don't often like to have an audience but today —" Her phone rang. As soon as she answered it she tensed again as if someone was pulling her strings from a distance. I wondered if it was Jennifer.

"Yes. No. Yes, I will."

"Jennifer?"

"Yes, she wanted to remind me that you're VIPs and not to mess things up. As if that cow knew anything about lab work. I have more knowledge in my little finger than she has in her entire constipated body." Duncan and I laughed. That seemed to ease Mara's tension.

"Okay, young lady, I need to draw your blood. Roll your sleeve up and stretch your arm out." As she approached I felt something similar to what I had felt both times when I had been near Jennifer. It was an awareness of them as individuals. It was as if each of their bodies pulsed in a different way and I had the ability to detect it without trying. Duncan didn't seem to notice anything special. Maybe he was used to it.

The multiple tests of my blood took four hours to complete. We stayed in the lab with Mara the entire time. Duncan watched her every movement. When Mara stepped away for a bathroom break of her own Duncan instructed me to watch her too. The purpose was to see what tests she was doing and to make sure all of my blood was used in the tests. None of my test results or blood should be removed or placed anywhere outside our sight. When the tests were finished she went over her findings with us. I understood about ten percent of what she said. Duncan, on the other hand, seemed to be fluent in lab jargon. He appeared to follow everything she said, asking questions several times.

"Are you sure it's Centurion?"

"Yes, I ran the test three times. I've only seen Centurion once before, in class, and I wanted to be sure. I'm sorry." Was that pity in her voice?

"Do you have an antidote? Anything that will slow down its effects?"

"I wish I did. It's rare and expensive. I don't know anyone who has ever seen Centurion first hand outside a class."

"What about a synthetic formulation? I heard someone in Israel was working on synthetic Centurion a while back."

"I don't know anything about that." Shrugging she looked at me as if to say something. She paused but said nothing more.

At the end, she gave the files to Duncan and destroyed my blood samples in the incinerator while we watched two steps behind her. We were so close that the heat of the incinerator made my eyes sting. Before we left, Duncan asked for the hard disk drives of the laptop computers she'd used to run the final set of tests. She walked us to the exit. "I won't mention the poisons or Centurion. If you ever want to visit, here's my card," she said to Duncan as we turned to leave.

"Thanks Mara."

Chapter 21

At the end of our visit to Tech Labtron we were both ready for lunch. Duncan had a place in mind already. This time it was a Peruvian restaurant. I had never eaten Peruvian food and was agreeable to the idea. Ten minutes later we were seated at the twelve table eatery.

Once again, my fast walking friend was able to communicate in Spanish with the staff at the restaurant. Duncan was at ease with the menu and asked about the special of the day. While the waitress went for our drinks he suggested I try one of those, explaining they were often the freshest items on offer. I agreed.

Since we left Pinecrest, I had noticed he was watchful. "When did my father make you responsible for my safety?"

"It's not like that Amy. I just want to make sure nothing happens to you."

"He probably gave you a speech about how it would be on you if anything happened to me while he's out of town."

"Something like that. It doesn't matter. The alternative was a security escort. I didn't think you'd like that."

"You know I'm not a fan of the whole security thang. Is that why you picked this restaurant?"

"In part. I thought you might enjoy Peruvian food. And, yes because it's small it's easy for me to know who comes and goes. I want to be careful and avoid any attacks like the one where your mom was hurt. For all our sakes." That reminded me that I had a lot of questions about the Weeia and their abilities. I realized that I didn't think of myself as a Weeia yet.

"Okay Fastman. I get it. On a more interesting topic, I'm fuzzy on who is Weeia and what they can do. Tell me more?"

"Sure. I'll tell you what I know. Beyond that there are many rumors and suspicions that may or not be true. Where do you want to start?"

"How many Weeia are there?"

"Well, that's the million dollar question. Nobody knows for sure how many Weeia there are in the world. In North America, The Elders have said there are about two hundred thousand Weeia, most of them in the United States."

"Wow. I didn't know there were so many of us. It's weird to think of myself as Weeia. All my life I've been the girl next door, just another human. Where do they live?"

"Many Weeia live in clusters like some of the reclusive religious groups you may have heard about. In the past, they would buy all the land they could in isolated places. They would put the property in the name of family trusts and build a community for their people. The trusts still exist. They pass from generation to generation without drawing attention to Weeia long life. Over time, the communities became villages and small towns. Weeia feel safe in those communities among others of their own kind. It means they don't have to move when they age or go away to have a baby. Most important of all, they don't have to hide their abilities from their friends and family. The down side is that they lose touch with humans and their ways. That can cause problems."

"What about big cities? Do Weeia live in Miami, New York, Chicago oh, there must be many Weeia in California. Nobody would notice if you were a little odd over there. They would just think you were in show business, an act. Being young forever is an art form in The Golden State." Duncan laughed. Large quantities of exotic lunch dishes arrived and we focused our attention on the meal. The problem for me was that everything was spicy and so hot I had trouble finding something to eat. In the end, I raided the bread basket. White rice and a simple lettuce and tomato salad saved me from hunger.

"I'm so sorry Amy. I should've mentioned Peruvian dishes are spicy hot." Duncan's enjoyment of the food belied his words.

"You're not that sorry. Look at you gorging as if you hadn't eaten copious quantities of homemade breakfast. I pick the next restaurant."

"Deal. Whatever your little heart desires we will have." Spicy yellow sauce covered the fish dish he ate as if he hadn't eaten in days. Since I had eaten everything I was going to eat I began to pepper him with questions again.

"Is there something different about Weeia?"

"Nothing like a vestigial tail, pointed ears or devil horns poking out of your forehead."

"That's no fun. So, how can you tell if someone is Weeia?"

"You don't always know. If a Weeia has abilities of the same type you do and they're using them in front of you, you might notice them, especially if their abilities are strong like a Medius or Maximus."

"Whoa, you lost me. What do you mean the same type as you do? You mean like speed walking and dreamshifting?"

"Kinda. Most Weeia have one ability. Some Weeia may have two types of abilities, a dominant ability and a lesser ability. Think of it as right hand and left hand abilities. For example, speed walking is my dominant ability." I knew asking Weeia about their abilities was considered rude but Duncan and I were friends.

"And—"

"And…what?" He asked with an innocent tone between bites of something crunchy, as if he didn't know what I wanted to know. The food smelled good. It was a shame it was too spicy for me to eat.

"Well, are you going to tell me or keep me in suspense?"

"You know already. Think." I was silent, scanning my

memory without success. I was about to say I had no idea and accuse him of distracting me when it hit me.

"Healing." My voice shot up with excitement as the waitress came to check on us. By then there was little left on the plates. Seeing my mood and the empty plates she must have assumed we had both loved the meal. She asked me something like *bueno*? To which I replied, *si*. She offered dessert and I passed pointing at my belly as if I was too full. It was possible they put chili on their desserts too, I thought. Duncan asked for coffee.

"You're right."

"Do I have another ability?" He shrugged. "If my dominant ability is dreamshifting what's my lesser one?"

"We'll have to find out. Abilities appear for the first time in most Weeia in their twenties."

"Maybe it's speed walking. Wouldn't that be fun? That would explain why I can go with you on the speed walks and not get sick." He laughed.

"What, you don't think I'm good enough to speed walk?"

"I'm sure you could be and it would explain things. You haven't shown signs of a lesser ability yet so you may only have one. If you have a secondary ability, who's to say that's not it."

"Does anyone have two dominant abilities?"

"You mean like being ambidextrous?"

"Yeah, like that."

"Clever girl. The Elders are double dominant. That's one of the reasons, along with their high level of power and desire to run everything, that they're Elders."

"Ooh, so if I had two dominant abilities I could be Elder. Wouldn't that be nice?" The scowl on his face said he didn't think so.

"You don't think much of The Elders, do you?"

"I don't think they represent the interests of the Weeia. Instead, they do things that benefit their own interests, their friends and supporters. They want to keep things the way they are because that's good for them even if it's not good for everyone else." I could tell he had strong feelings about The Elders and I wanted to know more, later. At the moment, I wanted to hear about Weeia abilities.

"I want to go back to what you said before, that Weeia have types of abilities. What does that mean? What types are there?"

"There are four main types of abilities, or henki: Emotional, Material, Mental, and Temporal. Can you guess where speed walking falls?"

"Well, I can guess where it doesn't fall. Not Emotional and not Mental— uh, not sure."

"Temporal. It's related to time bending. Time slows down for me and it goes faster for everyone else when I speed walk. That's why others can't see me. It's also why I can dodge bullets."

"Funny. What about healing yourself? Which type of ability does that fall under?"

"Any guess?"

"Nope."

"It's the same type of ability that rules your dreams, Material. The odd thing is that until I was shot, my healing ability was all but dormant. I could heal small cuts and bruises, nothing big like that day at the beach."

"It's a good thing I'm around to boost your healing abilities then. Although on the other hand, I guess if I hadn't been there you wouldn't have been shot in the first place." An idea occurred to me that could solve our problems.

"If Weeia with Material abilities can heal themselves can they heal others?"

"I see where you're going. A powerful Material henki, like your father, can heal others. Abilities manifest in different ways in different people depending on the gifts they're born with, how good they are at using them, how much they practice, and how powerful they are. I don't know what your father's abilities are. As the enforcer I'd be surprised if healing others is his super power."

"Could you heal Mom?"

"I doubt I could heal anyone else. My primary ability is Medius, my secondary isn't likely to be strong enough. I'd need to be Maximus."

"What about me? You said dreamshifting abilities are Material. If my second ability was healing— ah, but I'd have to be Maximus like my father, right?" He nodded.

By now the restaurant was emptying. Noticing we were ready, the waitress brought the check.

Chapter 22

With the lab tests and lunch behind us it was time to buy some clothes. I was looking forward to it. It was not so much that I liked shopping as that I thought it would be fun with Duncan. I had nothing to wear other than the clothes I had on, and my old outfit which was ready to be retired. Shoes were a must for me and we both needed swimsuits if we were going to take advantage of the pool. It was the first time I had stayed in a house with its own pool. If I had anything to do with it we were going for a swim that afternoon. It would be hard for him to wiggle his way out of the shopping shy of leaving me at the mall and picking me up later. Given his self appointed role of guardian I doubted he'd agree to that.

There were a lot of options for our shopping excursion. We decided to find a place near Pinecrest. That way when we finished we would be near the house and avoid rush hour traffic. The city's growth outpaced its highways. All day, the highways and main roads were congested. During rush hour the roads looked like parking lots. On the way south, Duncan picked up voicemail messages and answered calls that couldn't wait. It was touch and go traffic and I kept an eye on directions as a backup to the car's navigation system. I had questions about the lab test results and the Centurion they had discussed. It was obvious Duncan was avoiding the subject so I gave him time.

We stopped at one mall in Coral Gables, the pretty neighborhood where Mom and I had lived for a short time when we first arrived in Miami, to buy a few things. We found the rest at a mall south of Pinecrest. As I had expected, shopping with Duncan was entertaining. We joked around and I laughed until my belly ached. We returned to the house with a pile of clothes, shoes and pool related items.

No sooner had we unloaded the car than it started pouring with a vengeance. Miami is famous for its sunshine and beaches. I had discovered it was also well known for heavy duty thunderstorms. The housekeeper had come and gone while we were out. After the frustrating lunch I had I was thankful that she'd cooked another feast. When we left the Peruvian restaurant, Duncan had offered to stop for fast food or anywhere else I wanted. The problem was that I was no longer hungry. By dinner time I'd be ready for Marcia's Latin dishes. I was salivating at the thought.

While Duncan took the opportunity to get some work done I went online looking for information on Centurion. All the results were about high commanders in Roman times. I'd wait until dinner was over. If he didn't bring it up I would. I had to know.

My good intentions to wait until after dinner melted away when I saw Duncan sitting at his computer in the living room. "Someone injected me with Roman high commanders when I wasn't looking?" There was a weak semblance of a smile on his otherwise serious face.

"I don't know much. I was hoping to ask my grandfather about it before discussing it with you. He hasn't called back yet. We should speak with your father and find out more about it. What I know for sure is that it's a famous chemical among the Weeia. I think it's because it's rare and expensive."

"But, you're worried?"

"Yes, I think it's probably what's making you ill. It affects only Weeia with abilities and as far as we know you started feeling sick after they injected you. I assume that's what was in the injection."

It was my turn to come clean about my suspicions. I told him about the red lights that seemed to trigger bad headaches and impede my dreamshifting. "Well, for weeks I ate what they served me and drank the nightly tea without concerns. As the days passed, I began feeling sluggish and tired all the time. Having dreams became difficult and sometimes gave me horrible headaches. I didn't feel right. I became suspicious that they were drugging me. I decided to test my theory. The easiest thing to test was the tea. I began faking drinking the tea and almost overnight was feeling more like myself. I ate less of the food just in case. After that, my meditation sessions were easier. That was when I decided to look for Mom while dreamshifting."

"Why didn't you tell me when I first saw you?" He looked like I had punched him.

"I'm sorry Duncan. I wasn't sure if they were drugging me and I didn't want to make you feel worse than you already did when you discovered everything that had happened. What would you have done? You would've wanted to help me and have me move out but I had nowhere to go."

I saw understanding in his face and sadness. "What do you think now? Do you think the tea was making you sick?"

"I'm pretty sure it was. But, I stopped taking the tea weeks ago. It doesn't make sense that I'm feeling so bad at night. I don't think that can be the tea. It probably is whatever they injected me with that night." We were both quiet, thinking. Then, Duncan pulled out his smart phone.

"I'm going to call my grandfather again to see if he knows anything about your symptoms from the tea. 'Kay?" I nodded, thinking back to those many weeks alone with Master Tse, Ping and Lala. The phone rang a long time before anyone picked it up. Just as I was sure no one was home a man's voice answered. It was clear Duncan and his grandfather were close. It made me wonder, with a pang, about my grandparents, not for the first time. After a few minutes of family related chatter, Duncan told him about my suspicions and introduced me to his granddad.

"Young lady, tell me what the tea looked like."

"It was dark red."

"Was it clear or thick?"

"Thicker than herbal tea."

"How was the taste?"

"It was bitter and sweet."

"Did it have any smell?"

I had forgotten about the smell until he asked. "Yes, it's—hard to describe. It was sweet, thick and unlike anything I know. I'd recognize it if I smelled it again."

"How did it make you feel?"

"I was restless at night, sometimes woke up in a sweat. The following day I woke up tired and with a bad headache."

"For how long, how many days did you drink this tea?"

"For six weeks."

"How often?"

"Every night."

Silence followed for so long I wondered if he was still on the line. I held my tongue with difficulty.

"And, now what are your symptoms?"

"When I go to sleep I wake up sweating, my heart racing and with a pounding in my head; then I feel like I'm going to throw up." Duncan had told me not to discuss my abilities with others unless I knew them well and trusted them. I didn't know his grandfather. I was tempted to blurt out that I had discovered the effects were related to my dreamshifting. Instead I waited.

"I fear you may have ingested a toxic substance. There are a number of things that could do what you describe. Most will be flushed out of your body in the normal digestive process. A handful have cumulative effects. A Weeia healer should be able to help." He sounded like he wanted to reassure me but couldn't bring himself to lie.

"The headaches are horrible, strong and throbbing followed by nausea. The light bothers me and so do loud sounds. What would cause that?"

"That sounds like migraine symptoms. Does your mother suffer from migraines?"

"No, not that I know of. What causes them?"

"Nobody knows. Something in your life is giving you migraines. You need to find out what."

"How bad are they? Will I get worse?"

"It depends on the underlying cause. Although migraines can be debilitating and affect your quality of life they can be managed. Only one substance that I know of causes migraine like symptoms and is so harmful it can cause death. I don't suppose you should worry about it. You wouldn't come across it in your day to day life. Because it's distilled from a smelly flowering plant that blossoms only once every one hundred years it's almost impossible to find and one of the most expensive liquids on the planet."

My heart sped. "What's it called?"

"Centurion." I looked at Duncan and he looked at me. We said nothing to his grandfather.

"Grandpa, who's the best healer you know?"

"Agatha Chi in Georgia. She's getting on in years and cantankerous as all get out but she's the best. She seldom leaves her home and I don't think she sees patients anymore. You shouldn't need her help. I think a few days of rest and Amy should be fine."

"If not?"

"Tell Agatha I send my love. She'll give you a punch in the teeth but she won't shut the door." With that he cackled at some old private joke.

After we hung up, Duncan's grandfather's words stuck in my head. I kept thinking that if I had been smarter, suspicious sooner, stopped taking the tea earlier, or had left the property before I'd have found out about my mother, and I might not have Centurion in my blood. When Duncan tried to comfort me, I was sharp at him. I don't remember the exact words I said before I stormed off to my room. It was something along the lines of I wished we had never met. I should be mad at myself. It wasn't Duncan's fault. He was being a good friend, trying to help me. It was easier and hurt less to be mad at him.

Later, after I calmed down, I found him in the TV room surfing the web.

"Sorry." I sounded like the coward that I was. I should have accepted the blame instead of being angry at him. All I could do now was try to make it right.

"Don't worry about it. We all have bad days. The Centurion sounds like scary stuff. I shouldn't have made light of it. I was only trying to make you feel better."

I felt like crying. There were so many feelings competing for attention within me. I was angry at those awful people for what they had done to me. Because they were dead now I had no one to be mad at on that front. I was afraid that we wouldn't be able to get Mom out of the coma. I was afraid that my father's enemies still wanted to kill me because it was an easy way to hurt him. Now the news of some freaky Centurion injection and tea that might kill me was overwhelming me. I had to look at the bright side. Instead of giving in to the maelstrom of emotions I said, "Meet you in the pool in ten minutes, last one in the water is a scaredy cat," before dashing out to change.

We were in the pool for so long that I had pruney fingers. But, by the time we got out I felt better. I took a hot shower, changed into new clothes and was ready to face the world again or at least Duncan.

Dinner, as I had anticipated, was much more to my liking than lunch had been. As usual, Duncan ate like it was his last day on earth. Apropos of nothing I said, "I think what makes me sick is dreamshifting."

"Huh?"

"When I tried to dreamshift last night, my heart felt like it was going to fly out of my chest, then I got the headache and felt like gagging. I don't think it's sleeping or regular dreaming, Fastman. I think my Weeia ability is what's making me sick."

"That's not good—" I was glad that he was too surprised to ask when I had found out and why I hadn't said anything.

"If Centurion only affects Weeia it makes sense." The moment I finished saying that I saw my father standing behind Duncan. His face was a grimace.

Duncan saw me looking at my father and turned around.

"How long have you been here?" I heard him say. I knew from the look of concern on my father's face that he'd been in the room long enough to hear the important part of the conversation.

"Long enough." His deep voice was more of a grunt. "You should have called me." He turned to Duncan who turned a shade paler than he'd been moments earlier.

"It's been a long day." I interrupted. "I only discovered today that dreamshifting is what's making me sick. Like you, Duncan didn't know until a minute ago."

"Very well, bring me up to speed." He looked tired in spite of his command. Duncan and I took turns recounting the events of the day, leaving out the shopping, argument and pool shenanigans.

"I know Healer Chi. She is one of the most experienced of our people in the healing of Weeia. I contacted her about your mother. She turned me down." Again I noticed my father looked tired, more than tired, fatigued. I offered him something to eat and to my surprise he agreed. While I put a plate together Duncan continued the conversation.

"My grandfather knows her. I think if I approach her she might agree to help us."

Not understanding why a healer would say no to my father I asked him about it.

"She does not like to work with The Elders." I noticed

tension pass between my father and Duncan. Figuring it had something to do with Weeia and The Elders issues I left it alone. There would be time for difficult conversations when Mom recovered. "It does not matter Amy. I found another well known healer who is discrete and willing to assist us. He will arrive tomorrow afternoon. I made arrangements with the hospital. We will transfer your mother to the house in the morning."

I was more than surprised at my father's speed and efficiency. "How? How did you convince the hospital to let us take her home?"

"I can be very convincing when I put my mind to it, and few humans can resist my will. They will release your mother into the custody of a specialist. Our healer is also a psychiatrist of world renown."

"Thank you." My voice, higher than normal, broke.

"Do not thank me yet. As I said when you first contacted me, I do not know if we will succeed. Tomorrow will be a busy day. I suggest we get some rest." With that he dropped his plate in the kitchen sink and walked out of the room.

Duncan and I hung out for a while longer watching a scary movie on television. Although he had his own room he insisted on commandeering the futon in mine.

Since I knew dreamshifting was making me sick, I did my best to avoid it. I was still learning about dreamshifting and how to control it. Knowing stress was a trigger helped. I quieted my mind before trying to sleep and focused on my own well being. I began to feel warm all over and to my surprise, I slept like an angel until just before sunrise.

I was lacing my sneakers on my way to a jog when Duncan woke.

"Early bird catching the worm."

"Go ahead. I'll be right behind you."

I headed to the kitchen in search of smoothie ingredients and a blender. Minutes later, bellies full of smoothie, we headed out for a jog. The chill morning was beautiful with the clear sky that makes South Florida so special. The dew on the leaves converted every plant into a bejeweled marvel when the feeble rays of sun struck it with the first light of dawn. The air smelled clean. The traffic free residential streets had no sidewalk so we ran on the grass. For the first time in days, maybe longer, I felt relief, hope and the potential for happiness.

Chapter 23

I watched Mom while the nurse returned with the discharge paperwork, as she called it. My mother, nine weeks and counting in a coma, looked calm, like she was sleeping. She was clean. The nurse explained someone had bathed her in preparation for today. Her nails were clipped and her hair combed. I wanted to leave the hospital and its smells of sick people and disinfectants as soon as possible. I had become used to the neutral faces the nurses wore most of the time. It was the pity filled expressions when they saw me I had trouble swallowing.

Peter Marshall, M.D., the world renowned psychiatrist and Weeia healer my father had hired, had called before we arrived, smoothing the way with the hospital staff. Around twelve thirty in the afternoon, they placed her in an ambulance. I asked to ride with her and they sent me away, claiming that for insurance reasons passengers weren't allowed to ride with their loved ones. I mentioned that in all the movies and television shows relatives got to ride in the ambulance on the way to the hospital. They said real life was different.

Duncan, my father and I followed the ambulance in the car from the hospital through the middle class neighborhood in southwest Miami, to Pinecrest. Once at the rental house, the ambulance staff settled my mother into her room. Sometime the day before while we were out my father had made sure the medical equipment Dr. Marshall had requested was delivered. We hadn't looked in her room so we didn't even know it was there.

To our surprise Marcia, our housekeeper, oversaw my mother's arrival. With an air of command and knowledge she instructed the ambulance staff, in Spanish, on what to do when they seemed uncertain. It was fortunate she was there, as they appeared to speak Spanish as their primary language. Duncan and I kept an eye on the scene until the ambulance people left. Marcia, my father explained when I asked, was a medical doctor with years of experience in her native country. Because she spoke only a little English she was not able to practice medicine in the United States. She was qualified to look after Mom. That was more important than any cooking or housekeeping skills. Once we were sure Mom was settled in well we left Marcia to sort out the final details and look after her. It gave me peace of mind to have Marcia with her.

"Everything went well at the hospital. I'm grateful for all the things you're doing." I looked at my father with deep appreciation. For the first time since we had met weeks earlier I was glad he was in my life.

"Let us see what Dr. Marshall has to say when he arrives. He is coming here straight from the airport." My father had a conference call at four that afternoon. When Duncan and I offered to pick the doctor up my father explained he had already ordered a transfer service. Given my recent migraines he didn't want us looking for a stranger at the crowded airport or driving back in rush hour. I suspected he was worried about another attack on me but didn't want to say it. He guessed I wouldn't be happy with a security escort. Plus we would have to explain to the good doctor why we needed one. He might refuse to see her if he thought it was dangerous.

It was better if the doctor didn't know The Elder who had dragged him to see a patient with little notice was my father. We were to behave as if the woman in the coma was my father's employee who was also my mother.

I was on pins and needles the rest of the afternoon. I was poor company at lunch and only managed to eat a small amount of salad. When I went to see my mother I was agitated. Marcia shooed me away, making hand gestures for sleep. I couldn't tell whether she thought I should rest or if she was telling me Mom needed rest before the doctor saw her.

Something about the doctor rubbed me the wrong way from the minute my eyes fell on him. It didn't help any that I was anxious or that he treated me like a child. He addressed his questions and answers to Duncan and my father even when I asked the questions.

After two days of intense consultations he declared his work was done. He'd healed her body. There was nothing he could do about her mind. When my father asked about another specialist or alternatives available to treat the coma he had little to offer. This was not a common situation, he explained.

"What's her primary ability and how strong is it?" Dr. Marshall asked my father.

"She has Maximus Temporal abilities, she can shift her consciousness through time."

"Ah, that explains it. I have only seen a case like this once or twice, and it's consistent with her abilities." The doctor began, "When a Weeia with this type of ability, like her, is confronted with massive shock and pain, her consciousness often returns to a happier time and place in her life. These retreats in time may start out very brief, but if the physical body isn't healed and repaired, the intervals can become longer and longer. Eventually, the patient's consciousness builds a virtual bubble around itself and lives in a loop of time from their own past, afraid to venture out and return to reality."

"In normal humans, such a retreat is rare and may require fracture of the psyche in extreme cases, but our special abilities give the Weeia options that normal humans don't enjoy. It's our strength and our weakness..." The doctor paused for a moment, unsure if he should continue. "In the only other case that I have supervised the patient never returned to reality. Over time, the body stopped functioning on its own. That patient died when life support was withdrawn." That didn't sound good. I kept quiet hoping he had something more encouraging to say next.

"I researched the phenomenon and found a case where a second Temporal Weeia was able to reach the patient and convince him to return; that case had a better end. It's the only reason we understand the process at all, the revived patient described spending all his time at a favorite park where he met his spouse, reliving the same day over and over again."

"It's possible that she'll revive on her own without assistance, but the odds are low for both humans and Weeia after weeks in a coma. Research has shown that talking with them and the touch of loved ones can increase the odds slightly. I'm sorry to be the bearer of such bad news." He went on touting his many skills and experience until I stopped listening.

Before leaving, Dr. Marshall asked that we keep him apprised of her progress. He added that he'd return to check on her in a week. I wasn't looking forward to seeing his unpleasant face again.

It worried me that Mom's appearance didn't change after she arrived from the hospital. She still looked like she was sleeping and didn't respond when I spoke to or was near her.

Chapter 24

That night at dinner, we talked about what Dr. Marshall had said about Temporal patients going back to happy memories. I didn't understand all the details.

I kept thinking that Duncan had Temporal abilities, my father was a Maximus Weeia and I shared memories with my mother. There had to be something we could do. I was not going to sit back and do nothing while Mom wasted away in a coma.

"I think I know what some of Mom's happiest years were. It was when Kat and I were little girls. We were safe and she always smiles like she's lost in space when she talks about that time in our lives."

"That's a start." There was little hope in Duncan's face.

"Could a Temporal Weeia like Mom to go back to those years?"

"I don't see how." Duncan was just making me mad.

"What's with the negative attitude? I don't know all about the Weeia stuff but there's got to be a way to reach out to her." I stormed out of the room, leaving most of my dinner untouched. Once in my room I calmed down. I knew it was not Duncan's fault and planned to work on a better attitude for the following day. I made a point of meditating to calm down.

I was too upset to say anything to Duncan when he entered later. He took up his sentry post on the futon without a word. The events of the last two days must have taken their toll because in spite of how worried I was for Mom I fell asleep. I dreamshifted and found myself near Mom still in her coma and suddenly woke up short of breath and sweating buckets. The inevitable throbbing headache followed; although I thought it was less strong than the past two times.

I quieted my mind and concentrated on overcoming the sickness so I could help my mother. Once again I felt a strange sense of warmth throughout my body and fell into a deep dreamless sleep.

The following morning, I was in a better mood when we went for our jog. I was thankful that Duncan too seemed to be in good spirits.

At breakfast, my father explained that he didn't want other Weeia to know about me. He preferred not to call in another Weeia for consultation. As it was, the healer would talk about the special call he made for the enforcer. While my father was willing to help my mother he didn't want to add more risk to our situation. The fewer people that knew I existed the safer I'd be, he said.

When I pressed the point about what we could do he mentioned that Weeia were able to work together, combining each other's abilities by forming a circle. I felt the first stirring of excitement. I cleared the plates from the table, set them on the kitchen counter and returned to the dining room. He seemed to arrive at a decision and concentrated for a minute before speaking.

"Weeia form a circle to share their abilities and power with each other to accomplish a goal that might otherwise be impossible for any one individual. Each member of the circle makes contact with the leader of that circle, often the person with the strongest ability or greatest power. A typical formation is for everyone to sit around a table and place one hand in the center, stacked on top of one another, or flat with fingers touching." He had us reach out on the dining room table to demonstrate. As I peeked at the expression on Duncan's face, it seemed to me that some of this might be new information for him as well.

"Each person experiences ability and power sharing somewhat differently, but almost always in the form of sensory input. For me, each henki has a different tactile interpretation, so I experience Mental power as a cool liquid, Temporal power is like feathers and so on. It is how your mind processes the influx of shared energy and henki, and if you share a circle with a particular individual more than once, they will become recognizable." He looked at me to make sure I was following his explanation.

"So far so good."

"The leader focuses on the goal and the others volunteer their energy and abilities. The power drain can be substantial and it is vital that the circle remain relaxed and supplying continuous energy or there can be negative results." Something about the way he said it made me shiver, it seemed like an understatement. "As you might imagine this requires a high degree of trust in your fellow circle members."

"The take away is to pick your circle with care." My theatrical mannerisms and tone earned me a tepid smile from my father and a half serious look from Duncan.

"Adding energy to your own takes some getting used to. It can give you a high of sorts. For the leader, it can be tricky to learn to use the abilities of an unfamiliar henki, but the mind can figure it out. The secret is to focus on the goal, not the mechanics. Our ultimate goal is to locate your mother's consciousness and convince her to return to our time and her body, assuming the doctor is correct and she is residing someplace in her own past."

"Ultimate goal?" I asked him, feeling my earlier excitement fade.

"That is correct. Sometimes people are not able to share their energy and abilities or the leader is not able to accept them. Since you and Duncan are polar opposites this might be dead before we start. You are both inexperienced at using a circle and your energies may not be compatible. Although he is of the Temporal henki, he has done no time travel. We do not know if his abilities can be shaped to do what you desire. Finally, there is the issue of your Centurion poisoning which may render this entire conversation moot. I just do not know if this will work at all."

I couldn't hide my disappointment at the negative turn the conversation had taken. My father didn't see the expression or chose to ignore it, giving me a chance to absorb the situation.

"The only way to find out is to try. We have to start small and work up to it. To be safe you both have to be completely honest with me about how you feel and the effect this procedure has on you as we conduct our trials. Do you both agree?"

Duncan and I, each with solemn expressions on our faces, nodded our agreement. At the same time, a twinge of excitement went through me, this was going to be so cool.

"Okay, there is no time like the present. Shall we get started?" My father adopted a commanding demeanor, one I suspected he wore most of the time at work. "Duncan, you will be the leader and Amy and I will supply energy. For this trial energy will be all you care about. Your goal is to visit the kitchen of this house at midnight last night. That is about eight hours back in time and will let us know if we can do timeshifting as a circle. Are you comfortable with and understand the goal Duncan?"

I couldn't tell if Duncan was excited, confused or scared, but he nodded and took a deep breath. "Yes, I understand, let's give it a try."

It took a few attempts before the circle began to work. Each time my father would have Duncan announce the goal of the circle and we would touch hands in the center. The first time I felt him pull on my energy I was so startled, I drew my hand back and a spark like static snapped at me. As I examined the small sooty spot on my finger I realized it was burned, and began to understand what my father had meant by "negative results."

"As you can see, breaking the circle has consequences. We are creating a power imbalance and unless the power is expended by the leader, it is dangerous to break the circuit. Although it is rare, breaking the circle while we are not present in this place and time can leave us stranded elsewhere." I didn't like the sound of that, but it was all so exciting and dangerous. The excitement appealed to me while the danger kept me grounded. My father's voice brought me back to the task.

"Let us try one more time before we break until tomorrow." Duncan spoke our goal and we took our positions once more. This time I was ready for the energy pull when it came and I could hear Duncan's surprise as he felt power flow into him from the two of us.

"I can smell and taste something like freshly mowed grass after a rain shower, with just a touch of ozone in the air, maybe that is the opposites power, it has a bit of tang to it from Amy. This is amazing, like nothing I've experienced before."

"Focus on the goal." My father prompted him in a soft voice.

"Right, okay, last night at midnight it is..." And just like that he was in the kitchen at midnight, judging by the clock on the wall. The scene was oddly distorted from my perspective, like I was looking down a long tunnel and seeing him there in the other room at another time. Then I saw the door to the kitchen open and saw another Duncan walk to the refrigerator to get a snack. He was so startled to see himself walk in at that moment that I felt him return to us and without warning we were back at the table.

"Woo hoo, we did it!" As I spoke a spear of pain lanced into my brain causing me to fall off the chair onto the floor. Without realizing it I curled into a ball. I heard my name as if from far away before I blanked.

The next thing I knew I was lying on the couch in the living room with a cool cloth on my forehead. I felt weak like a kitten and a bit nauseous when I tried to sit up. Watching them wolf down giant Marcia size sandwiches didn't help. "Where's mine?"

Duncan vanished into the kitchen for a few minutes and returned with a pork sandwich and plantains on a plate and a large glass of water. I started with the water and instantly felt better, even hungry. I surprised myself with my appetite polishing off more food than I normally would in an entire day. "Clearly this circle stuff is an energy burner." Both of them were looking at me with concern as I tucked into the food.

"I am happy to see your appetite is still good. Get some rest and we will talk more tomorrow." That was all that my father said before he headed to the other end of the house to get his things. I heard a car starting out front and then he was gone.

Duncan was direct. "What happened there? One minute you were whooping with joy and the next you were on the floor in pain, and then you passed out."

"I think it may have been the Centurion." It was the only answer I had for him and it left me feeling a bit despondent and sorry for myself.

"I need some time to think, thanks for bringing me the food." With that I went out by the pool and sat in a lounger to ponder my situation. I remembered how well I had slept after quieting my mind the night before and it seemed worth trying again. I stayed with it for several hours. The sensation of warmth increased until it was almost unbearable, yet it hurt in a good way like yanking off a big scab to find the skin healed and pink underneath. I awoke soaked in perspiration and exhausted. The biggest surprise was that I was hungry again. I decided to shower and get cleaned up before visiting the kitchen.

"What were you doing out there?" As I headed back into the house Duncan caught up with me. "I woke up feeling the batjar from where I was napping in the television room. It seems like forever since it has been that strong. I felt an annoying buzzing in my ears and goose bumps on my back."

"Just meditating and trying to get better. I'm going to take a quick shower and grab a bite to eat, care to join me?" Knowing full well what the answer to that question was going to be, I didn't even bother to wait for a reply.

The next morning, my father was reluctant to even discuss further circle tests.

"But I had this amazing healing session in the afternoon; I think I overcame the Centurion. Today I don't even feel the slightest effects from it. Look, the burn on my finger is healed too."

"I am sorry Amy, but Centurion is— very tricky to heal, even for the most powerful healers." I figured he meant to say almost impossible and stopped himself.

"So are we supposed to just give up, when we're this close to getting the hang of the circle?" I was angry.

"How can you ask me to risk your life and health to try something that we do not even know for sure will work? Who could make such a choice with their daughter and wife? Your mother would never forgive me if we were able to save her at the cost of your life."

"Fair enough, I'll prove it; you seem to need more coffee." I closed my eyes, reached out with my mind and filled his cup on the table from the pot in the kitchen. I was thankful when not a twinge of pain followed.

He stared at his cup and said nothing.

"If we could go back to where she is I know I can convince her to return. I'll tell her she's healed and that I need her here in the present. She won't leave me alone if she has a choice. We're all well rested. We can do this, I'm sure of it." I was confident.

"You want to try again now?" Duncan looked at me like I had lost my marbles.

"We still have to do more trials before we look for your mother, Amy." My father reminded me and sighed. At that moment I realized just how tired and drawn he looked. "Better now than after Marcia gets here." He couldn't deny I was right in spite of his concerns for my health. We cleared the breakfast plates and locked the dining room door in case Marcia arrived early.

"This time, I will lead and we will see if I can timeshift by borrowing Duncan's ability. We will go back to the day we all met, agreed?" Duncan and I nodded and I felt that same shiver of excitement.

As soon as we settled down in our positions at the table my father pulled energy from us both. This time it was more abrupt than the first time. I could see from the look on his face that it was working even before I saw that strange, tunnel like distortion and our initial meeting on the street, months earlier. It was strange to see myself from that perspective jogging down the street toward the meeting that would change my whole life. When it ended we were back at the table as if nothing extraordinary had taken place. As we broke the connection, they both stared at me.

"Are you okay?" My father's concern showed on his faced as he asked me. At the same time, I got the impression the moment we had seen had meaning for him as well. I waited for the stab of pain to wreak its vengeance on me for the expenditure of power. It never did.

"So far so good. Is anyone else hungry?" I pointed to them as we heard Marcia arrive.

"It would be better to try again when we are alone tonight." With that my father left the room.

Marcia was happy to oblige us with a large breakfast, in spite of seeing dishes from our earlier meal. She must have thought we were part hobbit the way we put down food.

"Second breakfast indeed." I turned to Duncan who was smiling. I didn't know if it was in appreciation of being out of the circle or at the thought of a second breakfast. I decided it didn't matter. We had made progress, real progress.

The day passed by at a glacial pace. While my father and Duncan worked using their computers and smart phones, I hung out by the pool. After lunch, I meditated, focused again on my healing. I wanted to be my best when we formed the circle that evening. I jogged my memory for the years where Mom might be, thinking back at the periods she liked above others. By the time we sat down again, I had spent a lot of effort narrowing the options.

"This time, Amy will lead us. The goal will be your sixteenth birthday, okay?" I nodded my agreement, thinking it made sense, but was starting to feel a bit personal too. I suppose he thought I might remember that date well.

Once again we took our positions at the dining room table touching hands and I announced the goal "My sixteenth birthday dinner." The surge of power from Duncan tasted like chocolate with a slight edge of tin foil. It must be that polar opposites thing again, I thought for a second. The energy from my father was like Marcia's tres leches, sweet and rich with layers like the dessert's cake and frosting. There was also the oddest maple syrup flavor there as well, not really a great combination, but somehow it all tasted wonderful in my mind as I gathered up the power they fed to me.

I was afraid that if anything happened in this test, my father would stop cooperating for my own good. I was restless and impatient. Without meaning to, I brought my memories forward and the next thing I knew they were more real. It was like watching a black and white video of my family when I was a little girl.

I could feel Duncan and my father's presence somewhere without seeing them. I found I could make the video go faster or slower, forward and back or stop anywhere for a closer look. Fond memories rose in my mind and I longed to linger. Knowing time was not my friend I kept going at a steady pace. I flew right past the original goal of my sixteenth birthday, and kept moving back. The sensation was similar to swimming without having to push with my body.

A part of the video now had color. It was crisper and better defined than the rest. Curiosity drew me. Mom was in the room, holding an infant me asleep in her arms with a young Kat nearby. Her face glowed with happiness. I felt like I could touch her. She looked up and saw me. Blinking twice she stared at me.

"It's me, Mom, Amy." The image that was my mother set baby me down in the crib and walked toward future me.

"Ames, is it really you?"

"Yes." My voice trembled. I was crying.

"How did you find me? Are you alright?" It didn't seem like a good moment to go into too many details.

"I'm okay Mom but I miss you so much."

"I know honey. I wish I could be with you—" Her face clouded with emotions, regret, fear, pain. I was not sure what else.

"You can. You've been in a coma. You had many injuries and the doctors at the hospital couldn't cure you. A Weeia healer fixed your body. Now you can return. Please Mom come back with me. All you have to do is hold my hand and come home with me."

She looked at me, doubt written all over her expression. "Oh, honey I wish it was that simple."

"It is, Mom. You have nothing to lose. Just try. Think of coming home. Think of being in your own body. Think of being with me. Please Mom. Please." We went on like this for a while. My energy was fading, I could feel it. I had to do something. I reached out and held her hand. She looked at me and nodded.

The next thing I knew I was back at the table. Duncan and my father were talking to me. They sounded far away, their voices distant. I felt a hand touch my forehead. Something cool pressed against my neck. When my eyes opened I remembered where we were. I remembered Mom. I rose on unsteady feet like a newborn duck, wobbling forward toward the door.

"Mom—"

"Huh?" Duncan's voice was beside me, his hands keeping me upright. My father, concern on his face, was on the other side.

"She was with me. Did she come back? Did she wake up?"

"What?" My words must have been garbled because he looked at me like I didn't make sense or he didn't understand them.

"I want to see if Mom is back." My effort to enunciate the words must've worked because they looked at me. Gaining regular steps I walked toward Mom's room. Duncan and my father were behind me as I squeezed through the dining room door. I was rushing with impatience and tripped. Before I reached the ground strong hands caught me and held me up. I brushed them off with a curt "thank you" and moved with renewed strength.

I opened Mom's bedroom door. She was in the same position she'd been when I had last seen her earlier. No, I thought desperation filling me. It can't be. She was with me. We walked back together.

Then I saw her face, her eyes. She was awake, tears streaming down her face.

Chapter 25

The days after Mom returned from her coma at the rented house in Pinecrest with Duncan and my father are among the happiest in my life. I knew things couldn't stay that way but I enjoyed them to the fullest while they did.

Mom's wounds from the explosion were healed. Because her body had been unmoving in a hospital bed for nine weeks it needed time to catch up with her brain. Dr. Marshall, surprised she was out of the coma when we called to consult him, prescribed daily walks, healthy foods, swimming and mental activities in increasing amounts as she was able.

She wasn't happy to learn of my father's involvement in my rescue or her waking from the coma. It was difficult for her to recognize his benevolent role. She was convinced he had selfish motives. While I realized that could be true I didn't care. I had only known my father for a short while and the one time I had needed him, for me and for Mom, he'd come through. For that I'd be thankful no matter what he'd done or threatened to do in a past I knew little about until recently.

I'd thought he'd leave as soon as my mother came back from her coma. He surprised me by staying. He was concerned for our safety, he said. I suspected that was part of the reason. He also wanted an excuse to be around Mom even if it was for a few days. I saw the way he looked at her when he thought no one was paying attention. I had noticed on and off during the days we'd been together that his health was uneven. Some days he looked exhausted and on the edge of illness. When he was around Mom he appeared to be in better spirits and health. Maybe it was my imagination.

Mom was upset to discover what had happened at

Douglas Estate. She was haunted by the thought that while she'd been in a coma, with her mind huddled in the happy past thinking I was safe and comfortable under the protection of well intentioned people, I had been mistreated, drugged and poisoned. It was little consolation for either of us that the staff responsible was dead.

One morning, while Mom got up to get something from the kitchen I picked up the newspaper she had been reading from the table where she left it. There was a short article about a gas explosion in Cyprus. I found it curious that the Local News would feature an explosion in Cyprus until a familiar name drew my eyes down further into the article. It indicated that all the occupants of the estate, the entire extended family and employees of the Assugranes Family, had died. It mentioned that the Assugranes Family were the owners of Douglas Estate in Miami.

As Mom reclaimed her seat I noticed her knowing look. She had seen the article too.

"They're dead," I said in disbelief. "All of them." She nodded. We both looked at my father sitting across from Mom at the table. "Did you have anything to do with that? Is that why you went out of town in the middle of everything?" I asked him.

His only response was an enigmatic smile.

"At least you'll be safe from them," Mom said. She sounded relieved.

When I mentioned my discovery to Duncan he agreed with me that it was probable my father had been behind the so called accident.

"Everyone who matters among the Weeia will know McKnight was behind it," he said. "Their deaths send a message to anyone else out there who might wish his family harm. It's like the woman he texted you about the last time to let you know the problem had been taken care of. Now that he's in your and your mother's life again he won't tolerate anything that might threaten or split you up again."

On the plus side of all the events of the previous weeks, my father and I had spent some time together. I didn't know what that meant for our relationship in the future or what it was he wanted from me that made my mother so afraid. For the moment, I was glad we had a connection, frail as it was.

Mom was doing well. Her recovery was speedy and promising. She pulled me aside one morning saying she had a surprise for me.

"I've had enough surprises for a lifetime Mom. Will you just tell me what it is?"

"Spoil sport." Sitting nearby in a pool lounger, Duncan chimed in with a playful tone. He lingered for a few days too. A well earned vacation, he called it.

"I understand Ames." She hesitated. "I managed to reach my brother Bob. I told you about him a while ago if you remember. Anyway, we lost touch for obvious reasons. He moved to Florida years back and I just located him. He was a bit stunned to hear from me, but he lives with his family in a small Weeia gated community in Palm Beach, a municipality in north Miami. Because of the recession several of the houses are empty. A house on a lake with a swimming pool just opened when the family moved up north to be near their daughter who will be going to college this fall. It's ours if we want it. There are colleges and universities in the area where the Weeia kids go and a modest training center where you can learn about our people and culture." She looked at me.

I had grown up, home schooled, with Mom and Kat for company. For a few years I missed other kids but in time I had learned to appreciate the place where we lived and our privacy. I had spent the past weeks, not including the most recent days with my father, Duncan and Mom, in near solitude. It would be a big adjustment to live in a gated suburban community with other Weeia where everyone knew everyone and their business. "He said it's a nice area. We'll be safe there."

"Sure Mom. It'll be nice not to look over my shoulder for gunmen for a change." I joked. "And, the pool's a bonus." She smiled. I had wanted to live in a house with a pool since I was a small girl. I should be over the moon with excitement. I was amazed at how little, in relation to other things, that mattered to me now. I was so glad Mom was back and getting healthier every day. I wasn't thrilled about the gated neighborhood idea or living in the suburbs. If it would put her mind at ease and help her recover I was willing to try.

Duncan was sometimes good at reading my moods. This seemed to be one of those times. "I'll come down to visit you when you're settled in the new house. We can explore the Everglades and hunt for pythons. And, if Florida gets too hot or too suburban you can always visit me in Seattle in the winter." He winked.

"Of course Amy. You can visit Duncan whenever you like." As long as you take a small army with you, I assumed she meant to add. "There's plenty of room in the house. He's welcome any time." I figured that option was more to her liking. I was beginning to think I'd be trapped in suburbia for the rest of my life or as long as Mom could manage it.

"This sounds like too much serious conversation for one morning." He picked me up and before I realized what was happening threw me in the pool. I gave as good as I got and within minutes he was, new shoes and all, in the deep end of the pool, laughing. Mom watched amused from the comfort of her lounger. My mood lifted.

I knew not everything was perfect. We still didn't know where my sister Kat was or how she was doing. I had a lot to learn about the Weeia way of life and my own new abilities. Things were a lot better than they had been just days before. Whatever this Centurion was it didn't seem to be knocking me out anymore. I was going to focus on the good things and figure out how to solve the challenges as they came.

Thank you for taking time to read
Unelmoija: The Dreamshifter

If you enjoyed it, please consider telling your friends or
posting a short review. Word of mouth is an author's best
friend and much appreciated.

Sign up to receive updates and news of upcoming releases
on Elle's website:

http://elleboca.poyeen.com/the-dreamshifter

If you enjoyed this novel in the Weeia series, here is a sneak peek at the next novel featuring Amy McKnight:

Unelmoija: The Mindshifter

Chapter 1

As I woke up in the strange room I remembered I had a free morning without any tests, class assignments or chores. I was away from home, free to do what I pleased. Woo hoo. I liked attending college and I loved the private tutoring classes I took in my community. Between the two sometimes the work got a little much. A break was what I needed. I turned over in bed pondering what I would do with my time in Miami.

The retro design of the hotel across the street from the Beach had looked appealing online. It was less so in person. Still, the location couldn't be better. Well it could but at much higher prices. We were in the heart of the historic Art Deco District, one of ten historic districts on the world famous Miami Beach, according to the brochure I had read in the lobby of our hotel while waiting to check in. It went on to explain there are three well recognized architectural styles in Miami Beach: Mediterranean Revival, MiMo or Miami Modernism and Art Deco, the most famous. It wasn't until I paid attention that I realized part of the South Beach, or SoBe, charm is its historic buildings and unique style.

Visitors and locals alike flock to the tourist neighborhood in the southernmost section of Miami Beach, an island connected by three bridges to Miami which in turn abuts Biscayne Bay and the Miami River on the southeastern tip of Florida. On any given day, and even more so on the weekends and at night, traffic is heavy on the MacArthur Causeway that links downtown Miami with South Beach. The well traveled road with stunning views passes several tourist attractions and restaurants, an aquaplane port, and a handful of private islands where the rich and famous have homes before bunching up in gnarly lines at the mouth of South Beach.

There, brightly colored sports cars, late model SUVs, banged up cars with noisy exhausts and everything between coagulates into a slow moving mass of air-conditioned metal and carbon fiber on wheels until the traffic lights that feed them onto the two roads that lead onto the island turn green. From that point progress toward Ocean Avenue, SoBe's main drag, varies though it's frustrating at best. We were in such a good mood the night before we made a game of navigating through the traffic to our small hotel.

I knew Art Deco was an old style revived in Miami in the 1980s. Lilly, who was leaning toward architecture as her major or minor, saw the brochure I was reading and added more information so "we would appreciate the area we were visiting."

Lilly said Art Deco became popular following an exhibition in Paris in 1925. The design movement was inspired by the early twentieth century western European design styles of Cubism, Dutch de Stijl, Amsterdam School, French Art Deco, German Bauhaus and Expressionism, Vienna Secession and others she rattled off too fast for me to catch.

What was interesting about this neighborhood, she explained, was that it was from the second Art Deco phase between the stock crash and World War II. Miami Beach architects were inspired by local images to create Tropical Deco with relief ornamentation of flora, fauna and ocean liners to remind visitors that Miami Beach was a seaside destination. At that point, Krissa and I exchanged amused smiles and the implied intent to forget most of what Lilly was reciting.

Among my choices on a Saturday morning was an Art Deco tour Lilly had suggested we take together. I was also considering a walk along Lincoln Road, a nearby pedestrian street filled with funky shops and boutiques, art galleries, eateries and a host of memories. Further away in a quiet residential area in Miami, though still on my radar, was Larabee Tropical Gardens, one of the best botanical parks in the country. Lilly had also proposed a tour of Little Havana, a Miami working class neighborhood known for its Cuban immigrant heritage and culture. I had spent a wonderful morning there once with a friend, walking by its small ethnic restaurants, Spanish language bookstores, Latin bakeries and botanicas, shops selling potions and saint statues for practitioners of Santeria, a religion with Caribbean, West African and Catholic elements practiced by many locals. Krissa, more inclined to comforts and shopping, had mentioned she planned to head to Coconut Grove for a self-guided walk and lunch if either of us was interested in joining her.

Outdoor daytime activities during the summer in subtropical Miami require sunblock, a hat, extra dark sunglasses, being comfortable with constant perspiration, not minding the occasional encounter with mosquitoes and large doses of enthusiasm. I was accustomed to the heat and bright sunshine so I had come prepared with room to spare. I was back in Miami Beach. There were so many things I wanted to do, so many places I wanted to go I couldn't make up my mind where to start. I wanted to visit or revisit all those places. The question was one of time and priority. Moments later my thoughts of morning activities were interrupted.

Knock, knock, knock. I wasn't sure if I had dreamed the

sound. I looked at the clock on the night table, eight. I had planned to sleep in a little that morning and even skipped my routine of awaiting the sunrise. For the past two weeks my schedule had been intense. I had been staying up late to study and train so a little down time on my first day off after finals was in order before I tired myself out doing touristy things.

The small hotel was clean and the staff was not unfriendly which wasn't the same as being friendly. I imagined hotel staff developed a thick skin soon after arriving in a place like SoBe, the southernmost part of Miami Beach. Every Tom, Dick and Mary Jo with dreams of a modeling career or entertainment industry aspirations in Miami spent time in SoBe.

When we first moved to Miami, I read that most tourists to Florida from all corners of the globe found their way to SoBe at one point in their trip to see the Art Deco District, people watch, walk the pedestrian section of Lincoln Road, rollerblade, go clubbing or just hang out at the beach.

If the supermarket tabloids were to be believed during the season, athletes, supermodels and celebrities were regular guests in the SoBe luxury hotels. Reading between the lines it was clear they seldom commingled with the likes of us. They were VIPs in the hottest restaurants and nightclubs, escorted in and out by security staff and whisked away at their whim. We were content to share the general location and explore the small side streets. Lilly had struck gold when she found our hotel smack in the middle of the best zone.

I had been to Miami Beach a couple of years earlier. My tourism time had been limited back then. During my brief visit, someone had tried to kill me, injuring a friend instead, and forcing us to hide first, then leave in a hurry. Part of the reason for this trip was to recover my sense of safety by returning to SoBe for a girl's weekend with my friend Krissa and her friend Lilly. After studying up a storm in my first semester at Sun University, I was ready for a fun break with my two college friends who knew nothing about my prior experience in South Beach.

Lilly and Krissa were even more excited to be on The Beach than I was. Krissa was one of the rare people who had grown up in Florida without ever venturing to Miami Beach. She had an easy going personality, creamy porcelain skin, brown eyes to match her medium brown hair and a slim figure. Lilly, a Chicago native, was also new to South Beach. She loved all things fashion, modeling, design, cosmetics and beauty. Given that SoBe was home to several modeling houses, unique historic architecture and many beautiful people she had been beside herself with excitement since we began planning our mini break.

She had a soft oval face, blemish free skin and early morning blue eyes. She was all curves and sighs surrounding a heart of gold. She cared not that her shoulder length bleached blond hair contrasted with her dark brown eyebrows. Explaining that adult blondes were like unicorns she said a woman who was blonde at heart had to take matters into her own hands or the hair dresser's. Every chance she got she wore fashionable clothes and high heeled shoes that were impractical and, if you asked me, downright silly. It made her feel good about herself; she would explain when I asked her about the foot and back pain the heels caused. She insisted she was used to wearing heels and it only hurt a little.

Krissa was Weeia like me. Lilly was, though we didn't hold it against her, human. Weeia, human like people with superhuman abilities, lived incognito in society. The Elders, the equivalent of our executive, judicial, and legislative branches all rolled into one council of our most powerful Weeia, enforced a strict policy to keep our presence hidden from humans. They were afraid that if humans found out what a few Weeia could do they would capture all of us and use us for their own selfish reasons. Their fears, from what my father had told me, were not unfounded.

Our population was small by comparison to humans. There were two hundred thousand or so Weeia in North America compared to three hundred twelve million Americans, thirty four million Canadians and one hundred twelve million Mexicans.

Lilly had no idea we were unlike her. She was blissful in her ignorance of these issues. I wanted to forget my Weeia training duties and university studies if only for the weekend. I thought it wasn't too much to ask.

Our plan was simple. Mornings we were on our own to sleep in, walk around, whatever. We would spend the afternoon together sunning our pale bodies and showing off our brand new bikinis on the most popular stretch of beach. Lilly and Krissa were thrilled about the beach time. I preferred a quiet uncrowded beach. The attempt on my life had been on the beach in SoBe so that part was less of a draw for me although they didn't know that. I thought it would be good for me to return to the scene of the crime to shake off the dark memories and make new better ones.

My friends thrill had been rubbing off on me and I was starting to look forward to some sand and swimming among the tanned masses that claimed a small piece of the popular turf for their own each weekend. At night, we would discover the crowded streets and nightclubs to people watch and maybe even dance if we felt bold.

Seemingly the knocking had been my imagination, or the person had realized it was too early for civilized people to be awake. I rolled over and snuggled into the covers with lazy thoughts of sun and fun drifting through my mind.

Knock, knock, knock. This time it was sharp, insistent. Lilly had a key. We were supposed to have the morning free. Who could be at the door?

Resigned to my new fate I got up and wrapped myself in the hotel's plush rainbow cotton bathrobe. It matched the rainbow design of the room curtains, bedcover and throw pillows. Lucky for me I wasn't hung over or the colorful décor might have been difficult to stomach in the bright glare of the Florida sun breaching through the large windows.

I opened the door to my hotel room after recognizing Krissa's face through the peephole, wondering why she looked stressed. What was up? She could've just called from her room. For a moment when I first saw Krissa I thought she might be bringing me a surprise. That thought dissipated as soon as I let her in. That was not how I had envisioned our girls' weekend getaway to celebrate the end of our first semester. She looked around as if searching for something then settled her gaze on me.

"Where's Lilly?" My friend's light tone of voice belied the worry reflected on her face.

"I thought she was with you. I haven't seen her since last night." We had two small rooms for the three of us. That was all that was available if we wanted to stay in the same hotel. We liked the hotel, the location and the price. We figured out a way to make it work. Lilly, the easiest to get along with among the three of us, would spend one night in each room. We'd spent the savings on dinner the previous night. We had left it up to her to decide whose room to share the first night. Since she hadn't come by mine the previous night I assumed she was with Krissa who must've assumed the same.

"I thought you were together." Although she didn't say it out loud, there was a veiled accusation.

"After the drive down and pigging out at dinner I was tired and ready to head back. She said she wanted to stay, called me a wuss. When I left, five minutes after you did, she was on the dance floor."

"I thought she had spent the night with you. Did you try

calling her cell phone?" Krissa nodded, concern creasing her features.

"I called her about half an hour ago after her tablet alarm woke me. Today is her father's birthday and Lilly always calls him at dawn to wish him a happy birthday. It's something she's been doing since she was six. She wouldn't have forgotten or overslept. It's a big deal. You know how she is." Krissa rolled her eyes upward. Yeah, I knew how Lilly was alright. If I was a planner Lilly was a super planner. It was an unexpected side of her. Given her like of what I thought of as fluffy, I had assumed before seeing her in planning mode that she would be flighty and a procrastinator. She wasn't. She had made time during finals to put together our getaway. She found the hotel and read up on the tourist highlights and hot spots in town. By the time we got in the car all the big picture stuff was sorted and booked. She had come up with the idea of free mornings so each of us had our own space if we wanted it.

"You're right. It wouldn't be like her to forget." I didn't think she would hook up with a guy like that. Would she? "Do you think she would spend the night out with some guy she just met?"

"Hard to say. She's more of a free spirit that way."

"Would she stay out all night without calling or telling us where she is or when she's coming back? You know her better than I do. Does that seem like Lilly to you?"

"No." Krissa was quiet for a moment before going on. "She's not the most considerate person, you know. She likes to be spontaneous. One time we had plans on a Friday night. At the last minute a guy asked her out and she dumped me by text. The next day we discussed friendship terms. I told her last minute dumps in favor of guys are no-nos. She knows I don't like to wait, and a no-show is a big deal. She's gotten used to calling when she can't make it."

Krissa kept talking, nervous. "Now that I know she didn't

spend the night with you I'm worried. It's not like her not to call." I wasn't going to add that I didn't think she would have spent the night out at all or speculate on where that might have been. Krissa was worked up enough without me adding to her worry, and I didn't know if it was true. "I tried Lilly's number and got her voicemail every time. I called you too. Your room number rang busy and your cell phone went straight to voicemail." As she looked at me as if to say "what the—" I remembered I had left my cell phone charger in the car and hadn't wanted to bother Krissa for the keys the previous night when I realized it in case she was on one of her marathon calls with her boyfriend.

"You said you were going to call Charlie when you got back to the hotel. I didn't want to interrupt you. I figured I could charge it while we had breakfast this morning." She crossed the room and examined the hotel phone on the night table.

"No wonder it rings busy. It's off the cradle."

"I haven't touched it since we arrived. Maybe the cleaning lady bumped it or the last guest wanted to sleep in." I would've been out of reach if Lilly called me last night. She could've called Krissa or left a voicemail. I decided I'd check messages when I charged my phone. There was no point in bringing up the possibility of a message and getting Krissa more upset at that point.

"What do we do now?" Krissa sounded unsure. She was normally a self confident person. She was the one that often took charge and presented options for us to choose. That she was asking rather than telling was a sign of how worried she was about Lilly.

"Let's think this through. If we give her time she might show up and everything could be fine. Maybe she made a mistake. If we call her parents they're going to freak out, fly down here and alert the police. There's no turning back from that." I left out the part about how if she was in trouble or dead it might not make any difference what we did.

"We have to do something." Krissa had started pacing across the room and it was distracting me.

"Give me a few minutes?"

Krissa nodded. I appreciated that she didn't ask why or what I was going to do with the time. "I'll go get your cell phone charger. While I'm at it I can pick up coffee for me. I saw a fresh juice place around the corner from the hotel yesterday. Want a smoothie?"

"That would be perfect, thanks." I handed her a ten dollar bill as she headed out.

As soon as she left I sat down and made myself relax. Minutes later I was meditating. Some Weeia like me have superhuman abilities. Many don't. There are Weeia who can identify a spice in a recipe or the year and grape varietal in a wine. A few see more colors than the average person and some can distinguish the distance and location as well as the source of sounds. Other still can affect someone's emotions, move things with their mind, travel without their body, or self heal; a powerful few can even control or kill humans and Weeia. We pass as humans because our DNA is almost identical. Except for a few hard to find characteristics we are in most ways like humans with special abilities and long lives.

My ability is rare even among the Weeia. I'm able to dreamshift, make things happen in my dreams that also happen in real life. In the past, I was able to locate a friend through my dreams while I was in Miami and he was in Seattle. I communicated with him while in my dreamshifting state to ask him to travel down to where I was and let him know my location. I was hoping I would be able to find Lilly in the same way.

Try as I might I just drew a blank when I searched for Lilly. I was able to dreamshift without difficulty but nothing happened when I attempted to find her. I was wondering what else I could do when Krissa arrived with the charger and the drinks. By then, I was thankful for the fruit and vegetable smoothie.

"Any new thoughts?" Krissa must've guessed I was using my Weeia ability while she stepped out. Asking about someone else's Weeia ability is considered in poor taste as is boasting about your own abilities.

"If we call Lilly's parents now and she's off somewhere having a good time there'll be no way to unring that bell. I suggest we try to find her today. If we have no news and have made no progress by this time tomorrow we call her parents and the police. What do you think?"

Krissa was quiet for a moment. There was hope in her eyes when she spoke. "Okay. Where do we start?"

"Let's walk around where we last saw her in case she's around there or something. We nose around the area a bit, ask the neighbors and anyone who might have seen her. If not we get some rest and return to the nightclub tonight."

We had little to show for our efforts as the sun ended its journey across the Saturday sky. From the rooftop terrace of our hotel we watched it dipping below the Florida peninsula's western horizon, hidden behind puffy orange and pink clouds. I couldn't help but sigh at the tableau. The temperature had peaked in the nineties in midafternoon. A shower cooled the afternoon to the lower eighties. That is the good thing in South Florida. It never gets too hot or two cold. For most of the year it's hot. In the summer, in other parts of the country temperatures are sizzling over one hundred degrees while in our area, even in August, they never pass the nineties.

Nature must've thought it was unfair for us to have all these blessings and no curses. To make up for our temperate weather she created hurricanes. Every year, the possibility of hurricanes hovers over our souls for the better part of the summer, like an unannounced and unwelcome guest that might appear at any time, threatening us with havoc and despair. Despite the weather that many visitors found trying, hurricane season and mosquitoes the size of small aircraft; soon after arriving I fell in love with the natural beauty of the area. Beyond the city itself, tourist centers and popular places, there are uncrowded parks, botanical gardens, unspoiled beaches, natural preserves, Native American lands, rivers, canals and the world famous Everglades, a huge swamp that cleans the state and reenergizes the environment.

I drank the last of my iced tea while I watched Krissa fidget with the zipper on her handbag. Earlier in the day we had spent hours walking in the streets by Heroes, the nightclub from the night before, with little to show for it. That micro area of the Beach was depressed and near abandoned. A couple of buildings were boarded up, others showed signs of construction to come and still others looked empty and hollow from the outside. In our excitement the previous night we hadn't noticed how forlorn the streets were. In the light of day it was easier to see the poor conditions of the blocks surrounding the club than it had been at night. If we hadn't been so busy looking for the place we might have noticed it wasn't a nice section of town.

Because the club was kind of isolated without neighbors there was no one to talk with and ask if they had seen our friend. We found no signs of her and no clues as to where she might have gone after we last saw her. Our best chance to find her or news of her before our self imposed deadline was to go back to Heroes later in the off chance the guy she had been talking to when I left might be back. It would be several hours before the club opened so we were killing time watching the sunset. Worry was weighing on us. Krissa's nervous tension was a tangible thing and I felt guilt for having left Lilly alone. Although my head told me it wasn't my fault there was a gnawing feeling in the pit of my stomach. She was an adult and she made her own decisions, but we were supposed to look out for one another during the trip. My gut told me something had happened to Lilly. I couldn't shake the feeling that she was in grave danger.

Neither one of us was hungry so we skipped dinner. While we waited until the club's late opening time Krissa checked emails and texts and spoke with her boyfriend, also a Weeia. As a precaution she had brought him into her confidence about the situation in case anything else happened. I meditated, trying to find a trace of any kind of Lilly. A few minutes later I had nothing to show for my efforts. After almost twenty-four hours with no signs of our friend we were worried.

"I was willing to believe, no, I wanted to believe that Lilly found a cute guy to watch the sunrise on the beach with. I let myself hope she was having a good time and forgot to call us. I was clinging to the idea even as the day ended. Now that we still haven't heard from her I'm convinced something's happened to her, something bad." Similar thoughts had crossed my mind earlier in the day but I hung on to the hope. Krissa's words broke the spell.

"I agree. I have this awful feeling that Lilly's in trouble and needs us."

"Maybe we should call her parents." I hesitated not knowing what was best for Lilly.

"Her parents live out of state. Even if we call them now it'll take time for them to make their way to Florida. That's time we can use to try to find Lilly ourselves. I'm no expert but I understand the first hours when someone goes missing are the most important ones. The more time passes the less likely they'll be found safe. If we call them they'll want us go to the police instead of looking for her."

"Can you blame them?"

"No, of course not. But, a few days ago, I heard on the news that a federal investigation of the local police department found 'indisputable evidence of widespread corruption and excessive use of force,' for the second time in a decade."

"The moral of that story is to rely on the police at your own risk."

"Seems like it. Anyway, the main reason I think we should hold off is that they'll be emotional and we'll give in to their requests out of guilt and because we're not sure we can find her on our own. I say we stick to our original plan. We look for her at the club and if by tomorrow morning we have nothing we call her parents."

"Okay, except I'm going to suggest that if after we go to the club we have no news we call her parents no matter the hour."

"Deal." Now the pressure was on. On the other hand, there was no point in waiting until the morning.

***

...continued in **Unelmoija: The Mindshifter** - Available on Amazon now!

***

Elle Boca is the author of the Weeia urban fantasy series about superhumans. The Unelmoija Series is set in Miami. In the Garden of Weeia, a novella, is set in Portland, Maine, and her newest Marshals Series is set in Paris, France. Elle makes her home with her king cat husband in South Florida. When not writing and creating fantastical beings she likes photographing nature and wildlife, pastries, movies, and dreaming of going on safari.

www.ingramcontent.com/pod-product-compliance
Lightning Source LLC
Chambersburg PA
CBHW020941180626
46814CB00003B/886